FLIRTING WITH DANGER

Before she knew what was happening, Khamil tilted her chin upward and lowered his lips to meet hers, surprising her with a delicate kiss. He reached for her face with both hands, cupping it tenderly. His mouth was as soft as velvet and lingered on hers, as he gently parted her lips with his tongue. His tongue was warm as it danced with her own, teasing her, exciting her beyond anything she ever could have imagined.

The kiss sent a tingling sensation all through Monique's body, electrifying and awakening every cell. When Khamil finally pulled his head away from hers to catch his breath, Monique felt as though someone had doused her with a glass of cold water. She hungered for more of what she had just experienced.

FLIRTING
WITH
DANGER

Kayla Perrin

ARABESQUE
BOOKS

BET Publications, LLC
www.bet.com
www.arabesquebooks.com

ARABESQUE BOOKS are published by

BET Publications, LLC
c/o BET BOOKS
One BET Plaza
1900 W Place NE
Washington, DC 20018-1211

All Kensington Titles, Imprints, and Distributed Lines are available at special quantity discounts for bulk purchases for sales promotions, premiums, fund-raising, and educational or institutional use. Special book excerpts or customized printings can also be created to fit specific needs. For details, write or phone the office of the Kensington special sales manager: Kensington Publishing Corp., 850 Third Avenue, New York, NY 10022, attn: Special Sales Department, Phone: 1-800-221-2647.

First Printing: August 2001
10 9 8 7 6 5 4 3 2 1

Printed in the United States of America

Prologue

Monique's eyes flew open, greeting the darkness. For a moment she lay very still, wondering what had lured her from peaceful slumber to total consciousness. She wondered why her arms and legs were covered with goose bumps when the room was hot and muggy because the air conditioner had died. She wondered why she was afraid to even breathe.

Something had awakened her. But what? A noise? A bad dream? She didn't remember any dream, but it wouldn't be the first time she'd awoken feeling afraid because of something she couldn't remember. Her cousin Doreen would say that she woke up suddenly because she was about to die in her dream. And since dying in your dreams meant dying in real life, if you woke up terrified but alive, you should be grateful.

Yet Monique wasn't grateful for this feeling. For she *knew* something was wrong. She felt it with each *thumpety-thump* of her furiously pounding heart.

Drawing in a slow, quiet breath, she finally dared to move, darting her eyes from left to right, staring into the dark bedroom but seeing nothing. But that didn't mean that nothing was out there, lurking in the shadows. Perhaps outside her bedroom window, a stranger was scoping out the house, trying to get in. Against an unknown attacker, she was defenseless.

The sound of hyper barking sounded in the night, and feeling somewhat foolish, Monique instantly cracked a smile. Mr. Potter's dog. Of course. The neighbor's dog had awakened her on more than one occasion in the middle of the night. He must have spotted a cat, the way he was barking hysterically. Either that or he wanted back inside and was trying to wake his owners.

How silly she was, thinking the worst immediately. All her friends said she had an overactive imagination, and they were right.

Content, Monique rolled onto her side, snuggling against her pillow, determined to let sleep woo her once again. She let out a satisfied sigh. An instant later, she bolted upright.

What was *that*?

Now, she knew she wasn't crazy. She'd definitely heard something, something that made the hairs on her nape stand on end. Glancing toward her bedroom door, she cocked an ear, listening for what had awakened her.

Monique's heart jumped into her throat. Oh, God. Were those footsteps she heard racing down the hallway? The front door closing? Or was her mind playing tricks on her? She couldn't tell, not with Mr. Potter's dog barking so loudly, but the cold feeling was suddenly back, and she gripped the blanket to her chest.

God, she never should have watched that horror movie last week! Her mother had told her not to, so she'd gone next door to her aunt's cottage and watched it with Doreen and Daniel. She'd regretted watching the movie as soon as it was over, and days later, she was still paranoid that some psycho would jump out of the closet and hack her to pieces.

Was that what had her so tense? Or was it something more?

Monique lay back down, pulling the blanket over her head. Her heart still raced, but maybe if she counted sheep she could calm herself enough to fall asleep again.

"Help. . . ."

Monique stilled. Was that . . . ?

"Help . . . me. . . ."

The blood froze in her veins. Oh, God, that was her mother! Throwing off the sheets, she sprang from the bed. The cool wood floor was like a splash of cold water in her face, letting her know in no uncertain terms that she was not dreaming.

As she charged out her bedroom door, she heard a car engine roar to life outside, and for a moment she wondered who was out in this fairly deserted country area so late. But she soon forgot about the car as she ran across the hall to her parents' bedroom. God, she wished her father hadn't left angry, that he was still at their vacation home with them right now, not on his way back to New York. Right now, she needed him. Her mother did. He should be here.

Her mother's bedroom door was ajar. With an elbow, Monique shoved it open and raced into the room.

And found her mother sprawled on the floor.

"Mama?" Her voice was a horrified whisper.

"Help. . . ."

The pale moonlight spilling in from the window was enough to illuminate a dark spot in the carpet where her mother lay, a spot that could only be one thing.

Her mother's life, seeping out of her body as she lay in a fetal position, her hands clutched to her stomach.

"Mama!" In a state of horror and disbelief, Monique dropped to her mother's side. No, this couldn't be happening. This had to be a bad dream.

She reached for her mother's hand and felt a warm, sticky substance.

No doubt about it, it was blood. Too much blood. And it was everywhere.

"Oh, my God!" Monique cried. This was real. Oh, God, too real. As she listened to her mother moan softly, she was so numb and afraid that she didn't know what to do. Then her brain began working again and she remembered the phone. She scrambled to it and dialed 9-1-1.

"Mon . . . ique . . ."

"Please," Monique said, her tone anxious when the operator answered. "My mother's hurt. She's bleeding. Send help right away!"

"All right. Can you tell me . . ."

As her mother moaned again, the receiver fell from Monique's jittery hands. She hurried back to her mother's side, knowing the operator could trace the call. Right now, her mother needed her more.

Hot tears streamed down Monique's face, blurring her vision. Monique took her mother's head onto her lap, softly stroking her face and hair. Even though she was hurt, and blood stained her long white nightie, her mother still looked like an angel. She was that beautiful.

Monique couldn't lose her.

"Hang on, Mama. Hang on. Everything's gonna be okay. You hear me? I love you, Mama." Monique leaned down and pressed the side of her face to her mother's. "Oh, Mama. Please don't leave me. Not yet."

And then Monique stretched out beside her mother, pressing her face against hers, wrapping her arms tightly around her body and gently rocking her, hoping and praying that she would be okay.

Hoping that she wouldn't die on her.

One

Sixteen years later

"Oh, my Lord," Vicky said, placing a hand over her heart as she watched the next model strut his stuff on stage. "I think I've died and gone to heaven."

Doreen whistled softly. "Mmm-mmm-mmm. He is the hottest thing I've seen since . . . Since forever."

Monique Savard shot a glance first at Vicky, a fellow model, then at her cousin, Doreen. Both women were clearly engrossed with the view of the half-naked model, enjoying every moment of this lustful pleasure. "Remember Hendrix, Doreen," Monique said, mentioning the name of Doreen's husband of four years, who happened to be a very attractive man, even if he wasn't quite as sexy as the model on stage.

Doreen snorted. "Hendrix who?"

Monique chuckled as she turned her attention back to the stage. She was volunteering her time this Saturday night at a charity fashion show and auction to raise money for the Brothas and Sistahs Community Center in the Bronx. Her cousin, Daniel, Doreen's brother, worked at the center as a counselor for troubled teens. Daniel had approached Monique about getting her and some of her model colleagues and friends to participate in a fund-raiser for the center. Initially, he had wanted to have the female models perform in the show, but given work obligations, Monique wasn't sure that idea would pan out. After discussions with her colleagues, Monique had come up with the idea to feature male models; most of her female friends were always hoping to find the right man, so she was certain more women would come to such an event. She and a few of the other models had agreed to volunteer their time for this Spring Fling event, dubbed the ultimate ladies' night; Vicky had come up with the brilliant idea of adding a charity auction as well.

And thus far, with the standing-room-only crowd, the event had been a huge success.

"I didn't know they made lawyers like that," Vicky commented, her voice dreamy. Half Hispanic and half African-American, Vicky had thick curly hair, honey-brown skin, and an exotic look that got her a lot of work as a model. "What I wouldn't give to see that man on my bed wearing nothing but those bulging muscles and a smile."

"Vicky!" Monique exclaimed.

"Like you wouldn't," Vicky retorted.

"He's not wearing much more than that right now," Doreen added, then sighed.

"Shh!" Emily, another model from the Cox agency where Monique and Vicky were represented, shushed her. "I can't enjoy the view with all of you making so much noise."

All heads turned to Emily, who, with her hands on her hips and her head tilted to the side, looked as if she were examining a precious piece of art. Which, no doubt, is what most of the women present thought of him, if their wild reactions were any indication.

His name was Khamil Jordan. Monique had made note of his name after he first appeared on stage; he received such positive response that he'd be a good person to contact if the community center wanted to do this fund-raiser again. Right now, he was strutting his stuff at the end of the catwalk as though he was a natural. Monique suspected his confidence came from the roar of female voices that appreciated every one of his smooth moves.

He was definitely attractive. Approximately six foot one or two from what she could tell, broad chest, slim waist, smooth dark skin, and eyes that said, "I know you want me."

Yes, he was attractive, and he was sporting the bald look that she liked. It suited him very well. Would she give anything to have a man like that naked in her bed, as Vicky had suggested? It had certainly been a long time since she'd had any kind of action.

Naw, she quickly decided. While he was attractive, the cockiness in his attitude told her he definitely wasn't her type.

She wasn't hard to please, as Doreen often said. Her criterion was simple—fidelity. Unfortunately, not a lot of men believed in that. At least not the ones she'd met or gotten involved with.

Certainly not Raymond.

Monique released a bitter sigh, then put the thought of her ex-boyfriend out of her mind. After his betrayal, she'd decided to concentrate solely on her career, and she didn't regret the decision. Without the hassles of worrying about why a man who was supposed to love you wasn't calling or couldn't be found, she was happy. She didn't have time for love and didn't miss it in her life. Unfortunately, Raymond was still pestering her to give him a second chance. It didn't help that she often saw him on shoots, where he worked as a photographer.

Doreen didn't understand. She was happily married to a man she'd met on a blind date, and she believed wholeheartedly in romantic love. Merely three months after meeting Hendrix, Doreen married him. Four years later, they were still lovey-dovey. Doreen affectionately called Hendrix her teddy bear, because he was tall and muscular, while she was short and petite.

Monique was happy for her cousin, but her own experience was quite different. She had seen her parents, whom she knew had no doubt loved each other, argue so often that she'd debated if it was ever worth it to fall in love. But life had a way of surprising you, and when she'd fallen for Raymond, she'd thought he was "the one." Mere months later, she'd learned how wrong she was.

High-pitched squeals filled the air, and Monique looked up in time to see Khamil shrug back into a silk housecoat. Clearly, he'd let it fall off his shoulders to thrill the women. Well, they were definitely thrilled because as he coolly sauntered off the stage, women screamed and whistled and shouted for his return.

The bedroom wear was the last segment of the night before the auction was to start. After modeling several sets of clothes, it was clear that Khamil Jordan was the star of the male models. Monique had no doubt that he would fetch a great price at the auction when women would bid to spend a night with one of the men.

"Ladies," the emcee onstage began in a boisterous voice. "Is it just me, or are these some of the *hottest* men you have ever laid eyes on?"

Exuberant replies, agreeing with the emcee, filled the air.

"Mmm-mmm-mmm," the emcee continued. "Now, I know you all enjoyed the show, but now comes the real fun part. Some lucky ladies will have the chance to spend a night with the fine men we've seen up here tonight. As long as the price is right. Don't you all start fighting yet." The emcee and crowd chuckled when two women at a table near the front jumped to their feet and headed toward the stage. "Seriously, though, this is all for a good cause: support of the Brothas and Sistahs Community Center, which does a lot of work with our youth. So, keep that in mind when you make your bids." The emcee smiled. "Now, the first model is Robert Hawkins. Come on out here, Robert!"

The women cheered as Robert strolled onto the stage, dressed in formal wear. His smile could melt butter.

"Minimum bid, twenty dollars."

"Fifty," a woman from the back of the room yelled before the emcee had barely finished making her statement.

"All right. We've got fifty. How about sixty?"

"Sixty," another woman called out.

Monique stood at the back of the room and watched the women place bid after bid for a chance to go out with Robert. In the end, he was sold to the highest bidder, a woman who offered two hundred and sixty dollars to spend the night with him.

Monique watched in silence as the next four men were auctioned off, the most expensive bid being three hundred and ten dollars. But as Khamil Jordan strolled onto the stage to the frenzied roar of the women in the crowd, she knew he'd fetch a much higher price.

"Wow," the emcee said. "Did it just get a little hotter in here, or what?" She fanned herself with a hand. "All right, ladies. This is your last chance. Khamil is single, and says that he hasn't had any luck finding the right woman. Now that's a shame. But I know—no, I'm sure—that the right woman for Khamil is out there in the crowd. Am I right, ladies?"

The women replied with enthusiastic screams.

"Okay. Someone start the bidding."

"One hundred dollars!"

"One hundred. Ooh, I can tell the competition will be fierce for this one. Can I get one—"

"One-fifty!" another woman cried.

"Two-fifty," exclaimed the first woman who'd made a bid.

"Wow." The emcee gave out a low whistle. "Two-fifty." She paused, then said, "Two-fifty going once, twice . . ."

"Three hundred."

"Four hundred."

Ecstatic cries filled the air at the high bid.

"Five hundred."

The crowd was momentarily stunned silent. But a low rumble escaped when the first woman said, "Six hundred dollars!"

"Six hundred going once, twice . . . sold! Khamil Jordan sold for six hundred dollars!"

The women in the crowd began clapping as the woman who'd won the bid did a little victory dance at her table.

Monique smiled to herself, then turned and headed toward the community center's kitchen where refreshments would now be served, and she'd be helping out in that regard.

The few times Monique had seen Daniel, he'd

been running around like a chicken with his head cut off, worried that something would go wrong. But now that it was over and thousands of dollars had been raised for the community center, he would be happy. Tonight had been a definite success.

Monique saw him approach.

And when she realized he was headed straight for her, for some strange reason, her heart did an excited pitter-patter in her chest.

"I'm sorry," Monique said when he reached the table. "We're all out of punch."

Khamil gave her a slow and easy smile. "Then it's a good thing I didn't come here for punch."

Monique gestured to the other tables. "We're all out of everything."

Khamil's eyes did a slow and deliberate perusal of her body. "I see the one thing I want."

Instantly, Monique's body stiffened, though she felt a strange tingle all over. Her instincts had been dead-on about Khamil. From the moment she'd seen him on the stage, she had figured him for a pompous playboy, and he was no doubt that.

"Oh."

Khamil chuckled softly as he extended a hand. "Hi," he said. "I'm Khamil. One of the models."

Monique crossed her arms over her chest. "I know."

"Yes, of course." When Khamil realized she wasn't going to shake his hand, he pulled his back. "I guess you do, as you were here for the show."

Well, he must have been admiring his reflection somewhere when the celebrity models volunteering at the event were introduced. "Yes, I was here for the show. You were . . . good."

A hundred-watt grin exploded on his face. "Thank you. I didn't know what to expect, as this was my first time doing anything like this. But it seems I actually have some fans."

It was a simple enough statement, and clearly true since he had fetched the highest bid, yet Monique found herself curbing the urge to roll her eyes. The man had done one show, and now he had a following?

"So." His eyes did that flicker thing over her body again, making her feel as if he'd just seen her naked. "Did you . . . enjoy the show?"

It was the tone of his words that made Monique realize he wasn't referring to the show at all. He wanted to know what she thought of him.

She shrugged nonchalantly. "Sure. It was a good show."

"About time, right?"

"Pardon me?"

"Men have appreciated beautiful women for ages. It's about time women had the chance to enjoy the same. I was happy to oblige."

Monique wondered if Khamil was so dense that he actually believed this was the first time men had ever performed as models. She was tempted to tell him that it definitely wasn't the first and it certainly wouldn't be the last. But she didn't. Instead, wondering just how full of himself this man was, Monique cocked her head to the side and asked, "Is that right?"

"I believe in equal rights." His smile said he thought he was a god among men.

"I'm sure you do."

"And if you've got it, flaunt it, as they say." He flashed a boyish smile to make his words seem playful instead of cocky, but Monique wasn't fooled for one second.

"So they say."

As Khamil's chuckle died, he emitted a low whistle. "Man, you are one beautiful lady, you know that?"

"Who, me?" Monique pointed to herself and played coy. "Oh, you're too kind." She wanted to see just how far the fool would go. Did he think she was born yesterday?

"I'm just pointing out a fact. I'm a lawyer. . . . I deal with facts. And you are undoubtedly the most attractive woman in this room."

"Thank you." She hoped her blush looked genuine.

"I'd really like to get to know you. How about we get together sometime? Maybe for a drink, dinner."

"Oh, I don't know. . . ."

He fished in his jacket pocket and produced a business card and a pen. Before he handed her the card, he wrote something on the back. "Here you go."

Monique looked at the white card with the words *Burke, Lagger & Weiss* embossed in gold letters.

"My home number is on the back. But you can always reach me at the office. You can call me anytime you like."

"Can I?"

"Yes, ma'am. Now, how about that drink?"

"Shouldn't you be spending time with the woman who bought you?"

Khamil looked over his shoulder, as if expecting to find her there. "Actually, no. Our date is next weekend." Khamil raised an eyebrow. "So until then, I'm all yours."

"Really?" Monique feigned excitement.

"Did you come with anyone tonight?"

"Friends."

"Not a man?"

"No."

"Good." He took a step closer, and Monique couldn't help noticing his distinctly male scent. "Then how about we leave and I take you to a great place I know not too far from here?"

"I'm sorry, Khamil." She deliberately pronounced it "Camel."

"Kha-meel," he corrected, pronouncing his name clearly.

"Khamil." Monique took a step backward. He was too close, and she was uncomfortable. "I would . . . but I can't. I really can't leave my friends. In fact, I should get back to them. We're volunteering for the event tonight."

"Oh." For a moment, he seemed disappointed; then the charming smile was back. "That's great. I appreciate a woman who gives something back. I like to give back myself. That's why I agreed to do this tonight."

"Mmm-hmm. Well, I really need to get going." She moved to step past him. "As you can see, this place is a mess. I've got to start to help with the clean-up."

He blocked her path and flashed her what he must have thought was a drop-dead-gorgeous smile. It was, in fact, a little charming. But Monique ignored that, just as she tried to ignore how handsome he was up close and personal. "Before you go, give me your phone number."

She stared at him, not responding.

"Come on." He winked. "I promise I won't bite."

Good grief. When was the last time a man had actually winked at her? Mr. Jordan was the consummate player, she was sure.

"Hmm?" he prompted.

"Oh, why not?" Monique agreed, with a wave of her hand. "You don't seem like a stalker."

A deep laugh rumbled in his chest. "No. Just a man who finds you fascinating."

"You certainly know how to boost a woman's ego."

"I speak the truth." He handed her his pen and another business card.

Monique took the items and wrote a number on the back, then handed the pen and card back to him.

"Mary," he said, reading the information she'd written.

"Yes. Now, I really do have to get going."

"Okay." Khamil drew his bottom lip between his teeth. "I'll call you soon."

"All right." She smiled shyly, then stepped past him, wondering if Khamil Jordan was the world's biggest fool.

When Monique entered her midtown Manhattan condominium, the phone was ringing. She dropped her purse off her shoulder and dashed into her penthouse suite. In the nearby living room, she grabbed the receiver. "Hello?"

The dial tone blared in her ear.

Hmm, she thought, mildly concerned. She'd reacted first, thought later, not even checking her caller ID. She hoped it hadn't been Raymond calling. She'd been avoiding his calls for three weeks now, and she hoped he finally got the point that she wasn't interested in speaking with him.

Monique replaced the receiver and dropped herself onto the sofa adjacent to the end table where the phone rested, letting out a satisfied sigh when she did. It had been a long night, but a successful one.

She allowed herself a small chuckle when she thought of Khamil, and what his reaction would be when he learned she'd given him a wrong number. The consummate player getting played. It served him right.

Once again, Monique lifted the receiver. She may as well check her messages. She dialed the access code for her call answering service.

After she entered her password, an automated voice told her that she had two new messages. She hit the key to access them.

"Hey, girl. It's just me, Doreen. I wanted to chat with you before you headed out to the event tonight. Oh well. I'll see you there."

As Monique had already seen and chatted with her cousin, she deleted that message.

The next message began to play. "Hello. I'm trying to reach Monique Savard. Ms. Savard, this is Detective Darren McKinney of the Ontario Provincial Police. I'm calling about your mother's murder case. Please give me a call as soon as you can. We need to talk."

A familiar wave of pain and nausea washed over her after hearing the second message. Every time she thought about her mother's murder, she couldn't help feeling physically ill, even though the crime had happened sixteen years ago. For two years after the murder, her father had been the prime suspect. Ultimately, he'd been cleared—rather, the police couldn't put together a solid case against him—and in the end, the police hadn't found another suspect. The case had never been solved.

Monique quickly grabbed a pen and pad off the

end table, replayed the message, then jotted down the number the man had given.

Replacing the receiver, Monique laid her head back against the sofa, and closed her eyes. The strange tingling that always accompanied the anxiety about her mother's death spread through her chest and arms, down to her hands. Her heart was now beating faster, and no matter how she inhaled and exhaled slowly, nothing made her feel less anxious.

Though her family had lived in Manhattan, her mother had been murdered in Barrie, a small city north of Toronto, where they'd had a cottage. They still had it, though neither she nor her father had gone there again after what had happened. Monique remembered so many happy summers at that cottage with her parents, especially the time she'd spent with her mother, and to go there without her mother would be too painful.

Like her mother, Monique had become a model. At the age of thirteen, she'd landed a contract with Elite Skin Care, and she'd done several print ads with her mother. The contract had been for five years, but her mother had died a year into the agreement, ending the job for Monique as well.

Once the police had officially dropped the case against her father, he had packed up and moved from New York to Florida. Perhaps the pain was too raw, the reality that he'd been the prime suspect too much to deal with, for him to stay in that city. But he'd received criticism from the media and his in-laws for seemingly not doing more to find Julia's murderer. Monique had wondered the same thing, but had witnessed firsthand her father's agony, and understood that his unwillingness to even mention his wife's name was his way of dealing with the pain.

Monique had reacted quite differently. She had

vowed to follow in her mother's footsteps, becoming a successful model as Julia Savard had been. She didn't care about the possible danger and had gone to New York, always hoping to find some clue about her mother's murder. For months, her mother had been harassed by an unknown stalker, and she felt that stalker had followed her from New York to Barrie. Monique and her mother had been in Canada for a couple of weeks, taking some time off from their modeling contract with Elite Skin Care, and it seemed highly unlikely that someone who didn't know her or who she was would have found her at the cottage.

Monique's cousins, Doreen and Daniel, had also accompanied them on that trip. Only Monique had awakened when hearing her mother's cries for help.

Already, the painful memories of the past were giving Monique a headache. Her father hadn't been so much cleared as dismissed as a suspect because of a lack of evidence. Even though he hadn't caught his scheduled plane back to New York the evening of her mother's murder, and had later said he'd spent time in a hotel after a fight with his wife and had planned to see her in the morning to patch things up, his story sounded fishy, even to Monique. But when her father had looked her in the eye and plainly told her he hadn't murdered his wife, Monique had believed him.

Monique's family had always been close-knit. But after the murder, her father had moved to Florida to completely escape the spotlight. Monique had gone with him, but for years all she could think of was finding her mother's true killer, so as soon as she turned eighteen, she headed back to New York to pursue a modeling career.

Her father didn't want her to move back there. Knowing there had been a psychotic stalker after her mother made him hate the spotlight, and he didn't want his daughter to suffer a fate similar to her mother's. And with the killer never being caught, he could easily obsess over Monique once she made it big. Indeed, now that Monique was a woman, she eerily resembled her mother.

But Monique didn't care what the risk was; solving her mother's murder meant the world to her.

It was late Friday evening, but Monique took a chance at calling the detective. She frowned when she got his voice mail.

"Hi, this is Monique Savard calling for Detective McKinney. I got your message about my mother's murder, and I'm anxious to talk to you. I'll be here all weekend, and early next week. If you don't reach me, let me know the best time to reach you."

Monique disconnected the line, wondering why the detective had called. Was there news about her mother's murder? Was there another suspect?

Monique was about to call her father when she thought better of it. Unlike her, he seemed desperate to put the pain of her mother's murder behind him once and for all. It was for that reason that he'd moved to Jacksonville and had gotten an unlisted number. Monique doubted the police had been able to reach him. But she was back in New York, where they'd once lived as a family, always hoping that there would be some break in the case.

Raymond had often told her that she was too involved in the case; in fact, everyone had told her that. They didn't understand. How could she ever have a peaceful night's sleep, knowing her mother's killer was still out there?

"Forget it," she told herself, knowing she wouldn't. But for now, until she heard from the detective, she could allow herself to hope.

Hope that the detective had good news.

Hope that there was finally a suspect in her mother's murder case. Because if there was, and if that suspect was subsequently convicted, Monique could finally move on.

Two

Her long, slim legs were wrapped around him as he thrust long and deep into her. The sound of her passionate cries, the feel of her nails digging into his back, made Khamil's whole body burn with the need for release.

She was beautiful. Flawless dark skin, full, pouty lips. Looking down at her beneath him, watching her expression of pure carnal delight as he made love to her, was more than he could handle. Khamil had been trying to hold on, but he couldn't any longer. . . .

Instantly, Khamil's eyes flew open. Though he knew immediately what the real deal was, he cast a quick glance to his left and right, confirming that he was alone.

He'd been dreaming.

About Mary.

One minute he'd been awake, thinking about all he had to do that day, the next he'd drifted off. And once again, Mary had invaded his thoughts.

He looked down at his erection and groaned.

"Mary." He said her name aloud, a smile forming on his lips. She was beautiful, no doubt about it. What he wouldn't give to have her beside him in his bed right now, naked. She had a somewhat shy demeanor, but he'd be willing to bet she'd be wild in bed. He had a sixth sense about these things and was rarely wrong.

Unable to sleep any longer, Khamil sat up. Though he'd worked almost eighty hours that week, and had participated in that charity event, he knew he wouldn't sleep anymore this morning. He was beyond fatigue to the point where he was wired and couldn't keep his eyes shut if his life depended on it.

There was a lot on his mind. He had work to do. It was always the nagging feeling that he wasn't completing the millions of tasks he had to do that kept him awake.

And Mary. She also kept him awake.

Khamil swung his legs over the side of his bed and dug his toes into the soft gray carpet. He sat silently, a curious smile playing on his lips. He definitely wanted to get to know Mary much better. And he wanted to find out if his sixth sense about her was right.

It wasn't as if he hadn't lusted over a woman before, but there was something especially intriguing about Mary. Maybe it was her beautiful dark skin or her arresting brown eyes. Maybe it was her dainty oval face, her high cheekbones, and those full, sensual lips definitely made for kissing. Or maybe it was her long, shapely legs. Or maybe it was the entire package. No doubt about it, she was definitely luscious.

Rising from his bed, Khamil gave his muscular body a good stretch. Mary hadn't called him, but it was still early. He shot a glance at the clock radio on his night table. Yep, it was very early. Nine-twelve.

Knowing he had a lot of work to do, Khamil headed to the kitchen, where he put on a pot of coffee. He waited while it brewed, turning on the small black-and-white television in his kitchen to catch the news on CNN. Nothing much caught his interest, so when the coffee was ready, he poured a cup and took it to the dining room table, which served as a desk for much of the work he did at home.

His briefcase already lay open on the table, the contract he needed to go over in a manila folder on top of other contracts. He took a sip of the coffee, then lowered himself onto the chair before the briefcase. Burke, Lagger & Weiss was a large law firm in downtown Manhattan that dealt with everything from civil lawsuits to criminal defense. Khamil had been with the firm for seven years, and dealt exclusively with entertainment law. He'd always had an interest in the entertainment field, because for as long as he remembered, he'd dreamed of being a musician. That was a dream he hadn't shared with his family. While his parents and siblings had known of his love for music, they'd always seen it as a hobby rather than a viable career choice. He'd never seen it as a career either, despite the fact that he'd always composed and played music on his guitar whenever he had some spare time.

Khamil downed the remaining black coffee, then placed the cup beside the briefcase. He withdrew the manila folder marked *Graves* and opened it. The firm preferred to deal with high-profile talent, but often it did contract reviews for up-and-coming actors or artists. Khamil believed that these very same artists had to start somewhere, and if in the future they made something big of their careers, they'd remain loyal to the firm.

Adam Graves was one such person. A talented actor, he still hadn't had a big break yet, and was willing to do almost anything to make that happen.

Including work for low-budget productions that didn't pay a fraction of what he was worth.

Khamil lifted the contract, then briefly skimmed the first page before setting it down. Emitting a frustrated sigh, he pinched the bridge of his nose. Despite the conversations he'd had with the producer on his client's behalf, this version of the contract didn't look much better than the last. If his client signed it, he'd be basically giving away his rights to future income. Yet when he'd talked to Adam the day before, Adam had been prepared to do just that, caring only about the exposure the film would bring. This was a vehicle to future stardom, Adam had assured him. Khamil hadn't bothered to point out that the last four similar contracts had gotten him nowhere. He knew that Adam wouldn't listen to reason.

Khamil had seen one too many contracts like this, one too many broken dreams. Independent producers, unless extremely lucky, just didn't have the resources to get their films the exposure needed that would result in an actor's being "discovered."

He went over the contract again, circling in pencil the clauses he wanted amended. He'd contact the producer once more on Adam's behalf, and see what he was willing to offer. He knew that whether or not the producer paid Adam a decent wage and gave him acceptable contract terms, his client was willing and ready to sign on the dotted line.

Khamil was en route to the kitchen for another cup of coffee when the phone rang. The first thought that entered his mind was that Mary was calling him. He hurried to the kitchen phone and snatched the receiver.

"Khamil Jordan."

"Khamil, you have been a very bad boy."

Khamil couldn't help rolling his eyes. Yet he sounded cheerful as he said, "Annette."

"You don't return calls anymore. And you're so hard to reach."

"I've been busy."

"All work and no play isn't good for the soul."

"So they say, but it can't be helped sometimes. This is one of those times."

"I miss you."

"Uh-huh." Khamil didn't tell her that he missed her as well, because he didn't. In the beginning he had, but she'd called too much, had seemed too desperate, and that had turned him off.

That and the fact that she'd mentioned on their third date how much she wanted to settle down and have a family.

"When do you think you'll have time for a break? You can come over and I can cook you dinner, give you a massage . . ."

"I'm not sure."

"Oh." She sounded disappointed.

"But if I get some time, I'll let you know."

"All right, sweetie. You know where to reach me."

She hung up, and Khamil held the receiver to his ear, listening to the dial tone for several seconds.

Finally replacing the receiver, he blew out a long breath. Annette was beautiful and willing to simply spend time with him, which he appreciated. She'd been great for nights out on the town and the occasional rolls in the hay. But lately, he had grown tired of her, the same way he had grown tired of others in the past.

Though his family and friends wouldn't believe him, he'd always had hopes of settling down one day, of starting a family the way his brother, Javar, had, of helping to keep the Jordan family name alive. In his twenties, he'd always figured he'd settle down one day—after he'd had enough fun to last a lifetime. In his early thirties, he'd pretty much had the same attitude. Though knowing he'd sown enough wild oats, he had been willing to entertain the thought of actually searching for the right woman. For whatever reason, the women he met and dated were good for the short term, but he couldn't imagine spending happily ever after with them. And in the back of his mind, he kept thinking that if he chose just one of the several women he dated to pursue for marriage, he'd feel as if he were in an ice cream parlor having just one flavor—forever. He couldn't do it. So, since he hadn't truly found anyone he'd cared to spend the rest of his days with, he'd stopped worrying about finding the right woman, certain that when he was finally ready to settle down, she would walk into his life.

But at thirty-eight, that hadn't happened yet.

He didn't know why the perfect woman eluded him. Maybe he was too picky. He knew that any woman he settled down with would have to have a career of her own, for two reasons. He spent so much time at the firm, a wife might get bored if she didn't do something fulfilling for herself. Also, many of the women he dated could only be classified as flaky, hoping to snag a wealthy husband, and he wasn't about to play that game. He'd be willing to give his wife everything, but she'd have to love him for him first and foremost.

Khamil filled his cup with more coffee, then strolled back to his dining room. Once again, his thoughts went to Mary. She was beautiful, classy, a woman he wanted to get to know. Yes, he was sexually attracted to her; there'd been definite sparks between them the night before. But would she ignite something else within him?

Maybe. There was something different about her that piqued his interest. Whether or not she would sustain that interest, only time would tell.

A quick look at the wall clock told him it was now just minutes after ten. He wanted to talk to her, and sensed that she was the old-fashioned type who wouldn't call him first. He liked that. Unfortunately, a lot of the women he met in New York were too pushy.

He hoped it wasn't too early to call her, but as he couldn't stop thinking about her, he figured he may as well.

He fished her number out of his card holder, went to the kitchen phone, and dialed it.

The phone rang three times, then a machine picked up. Khamil was about to hang up, then decided to leave a message.

"Thank you for calling Tony's Pizzeria," a male voice with a light Italian accent began. "Unfortunately, we're closed right now. Our hours of operation are from twelve noon to one A.M., seven days a week. Please call back during that time."

Khamil looked at the receiver with confusion, then hung up the phone. He frowned. Maybe he'd dialed the wrong number. He dialed again.

Again, he got the same message.

Hanging up the phone, he leaned a hip against the kitchen counter. Something didn't feel right about this. Had Mary accidentally given him the wrong number? Or had she chosen to give him her work number?

A pizzeria? Did Mary work at a pizzeria? For some reason, Khamil couldn't picture that.

Oh well. He'd call back in a couple of hours and hopefully speak to her then.

Monique didn't exactly feel like being at this fitting so early on a Sunday morning. One, she was still tired from last night, and two, she wanted to be home in case the detective called.

She'd tried his line again, again getting a message. She wouldn't have expected a call until Monday, but he had called her on the weekend, so she figured that perhaps he was working weekend hours.

Oh well.

"Huh, Monique?"

At the sound of her name, Monique turned and faced Vicky, who was sitting in the small room waiting with her and a couple of other models from their agency.

"Pardon me?"

Vicky held up a magazine and said, "Okay. I'll read this again. If you were walking along Broadway and found a wad of one-hundred-dollar bills, would, you, A, go immediately to the police and turn the money in, B, donate it to the charity of your choice, or, C, call your travel agent and make plans for the vacation of a lifetime?"

"Is there anything to identify who the money belongs to?" Heidi, another model, asked.

"Nope," Vicky replied.

"Then I'd donate it to the charity of my choice," Heidi answered. "Me."

Monique smirked as she shook her head. "You are too much, girl."

"It's true. If anyone can use the money, I can."

"For another pair of Armani blue jeans?"

"Hey, I don't work as much as you two, remember?"

"You're hardly starving," Monique countered.

"Still, if someone's dumb enough to drop a wad of hundreds, they obviously don't need the money."

Monique chuckled along with her friends, starting to feel better. Maybe it wasn't such a bad thing being out this morning. All last night, her mind had replayed the horror of the night she had found her mother dying, and it was nice having a reprieve from that memory, even if only for a short time.

"Hey," Heidi said, looking at Monique. "Guess who I saw yesterday."

Monique shrugged. "I don't know."

"Raymond. He asked me if I know what's up with you. Says he hasn't seen you around for a while."

Raymond. He'd been calling her, but thankfully, her caller ID enabled her to screen his calls. She had no interest in talking to him, not after what he'd done.

"Our paths haven't crossed, that's all."

"Well, when I told him you'd be working with me on this spread, he told me to tell you to call him."

"Thanks," Monique replied softly. She didn't discuss her personal life with her colleagues. Only Vicky and a couple of the other models she considered friends knew she'd been involved with Raymond. Vicky had shared Monique's concern that the man had started acting a little too clingy, obsessed even. Even though he knew Monique was a busy fashion model, he wanted an account of where she was at all times and who she'd spent her time with. He always said this was out of concern for her, that he wanted to know if any men got out of line with her, but Monique knew it was more. Though she and Raymond had only been seeing each other a few months at the time, he seemed to feel he owned her.

Monique looked at Vicky, and she and Vicky shared a knowing look; then Vicky changed the subject. "Well, if I found a wad of hundreds, I have to admit, I'd be calling my travel agent to book the vacation of a lifetime."

"How many times have you been around the world?" Monique asked her friend, giving her a disapproving look.

"True. Okay, I'd turn it in. Isn't it true that after a certain amount of time, if the money remains unclaimed, you can keep it?"

"As far as I know," Heidi said.

"Then I'd turn it in and hope that no one came to collect," Vicky said, then smiled.

All the women shared a laugh.

Yeah, this was better than being at home, thinking about her mother's unsolved murder.

Fifteen minutes after noon, Khamil dialed the number Mary had given him once more.

"Tony's Pizzeria."

Khamil nestled the receiver between his chin and shoulder. "Hi. Uh, I'm looking for someone." He was convinced now that Mary had given him her work number. "I believe she works at your business."

"What's her name?"

"Mary."

"Mary? No one works here by the name of Mary."

"Are you sure?" Khamil asked. "Beautiful black woman. Tall and slim."

"Uh, no. She definitely doesn't work here. Maybe you took the number down wrong."

"No. She wrote it down."

The woman chuckled, and that said it all.

"Sorry to bother you," Khamil quickly said.

"I can't give you Mary, but I can give you a pizza."

"No. Thanks. Have a good day." Khamil hung up, but not before he heard the woman begin to relay the story of how some woman had duped him.

So, it was like that. Mary had given him a fake number. He'd bet double or nothing that her name wasn't Mary either.

He'd been played.

Three

Bright and early Monday morning, Monique got the call she was waiting for. Before the phone could ring a second time, she grabbed the receiver.

"Hello?"

"Ms. Savard?"

Monique sat up. "Yes, this is she."

"Hello. This is Detective McKinney of the Ontario Provincial Police."

"Hello."

"The reason I'm calling is about your mother's unsolved murder case. The O.P.P. has put together a task force to deal with what we call cold cases, cases of a serious nature that have remained unsolved for many years. Your mother's case is one of them."

Monique's heart fluttered. "Years ago, you never found any suspects, other than my father. What are the chances that, so many years after the fact, you'll actually be able to solve the crime?"

"One of the best things we have going for us now is DNA technology, which allows us to rule out previous suspects, or in fact confirm that they could have committed the crime."

"I see."

"Forensic scientists will be evaluating the samples we have on file to see if in fact they can still be used with any degree of accuracy. In the meantime, I'll be going over all the evidence that was collected regarding this case, including statements of witnesses. I understand you were the one who found your mother."

"Yes." Monique's voice was barely more than a croak.

"I may need to question you again in respect to what happened that night. And of course, if anything comes to mind that you realize you may have forgotten then, feel free to call me."

"It was so long ago."

"I realize that, but one never knows. Also, we'll be publicizing the cases we're reopening, so there's always the chance that witnesses who didn't come forward before may feel compelled to come forward now."

"I never thought of that."

"In fact, *America's Most Wanted* would like to profile this case on an upcoming episode they're doing featuring crimes in Canada. Because it was such a high-profile case—"

"Yes, I understand. And I think it's a great idea."

"Good. Now, is everyone who was in some way involved in the investigation back then, in terms of your family members, still alive?"

"My father's still alive. My aunt. My uncle. Yes, all of them."

"I may need to talk with them as well, depending on how the DNA testing goes."

"I'll let them know."

"Great." The detective paused. "All right. That's all for now. I basically wanted to get in touch with you and let you know what was going on, before you heard about it in the media, of course."

"Thank you." Monique began to hope. "And I appreciate this."

"Hopefully we'll be able to get closure for your family once and for all."

"Yes, hopefully," Monique agreed, then hung up, allowing herself to experience real hope for the first time in several years.

The moment Monique walked into the women's clothing section of the department store where Doreen worked, Doreen saw her. A huge smile spread on her cousin's face.

Monique forced a smile as she sauntered toward Doreen. "Hey, you."

Doreen's smile instantly fell into a frown. "Uh-oh. What's wrong?"

"Nothing," Monique replied, giving Doreen a brief hug.

Doreen stepped back from Monique and gave her a skeptical look. "Come on. I know you better than anyone. There's definitely something bothering you."

Monique glanced away, strolling around a rack of cashmere sweaters to her right.

Doreen followed her. "Monique, I don't think you came here to shop for new clothes."

Stopping abruptly, Monique faced her cousin. "You're right. I didn't."

"All right. Then tell me what's up."

Not only was Doreen her cousin, she was Monique's best friend. They could discuss anything, even if they didn't always agree. "I got a call today from a police officer in Toronto. He said they're re-opening my mother's murder case."

Doreen's eyes first narrowed, then widened, in surprise. "What?"

Monique blew out a weary breath. Ever since learning the news, she felt both a sense of fear and optimism. "I don't know why, but the detective said he thinks the new DNA technology may help solve this case."

"Wow." Doreen shook her head in amazement. Then she looked Monique squarely in the eye. "So, this is a good thing, right?"

"I think so."

"Then why don't you seem happy?"

"No reason in particular." Monique shrugged. "It's just not a pleasant subject."

"If you're worried about the DNA evidence—"

"The DNA evidence will exonerate my father," Monique interjected.

A hint of doubt passed over Doreen's face, which immediately put Monique on edge. "My father did not kill my mother, Doreen."

"I . . ." Doreen's voice trailed as she glanced away. After a moment, she faced Monique again. "I know you believe that."

"I *know* that, Doreen. No one knew my father better than my mother and I. Yes, they had their problems, but no, he never would have killed her." Part of her parents' problems was the fact that her mother had worked so much, and not spent enough time with her father, as far as he was concerned. Still, Monique was certain he'd loved her. In fact, he'd never remarried since her death. "He worshipped the ground she walked on," Monique concluded.

"Oh, Monique," Doreen began. "I'm not saying he *did* do it, but you have to acknowledge the possibility—"

"There is no possibility," Monique quickly responded.

Doreen was quiet, and Monique looked at her, but

she couldn't read what she was thinking. Doreen had pointed out to her time and again that most women were hurt or killed by men they knew, mostly lovers or husbands, as opposed to strangers. And while Monique knew that to be true, she also knew it wasn't in this case. She only wished her cousin had her back in this situation. Instead, Doreen probably thought she was crazy, a daughter who stubbornly refused to believe her father could commit such a horrible crime.

"What did the police say?" Doreen asked after a while.

"The detective said that recently, they've reopened a bunch of old homicide cases. Cold cases, they're called. Cases that were never solved years ago. There's a squad specifically dedicated to investigating these old crimes—the cold squad."

"I hear that's popular these days."

Monique nodded. "With my mother's case, they'll be reviewing everything, all the witness statements, evidence, et cetera. Hopefully fresh eyes can come up with something the original detectives missed." Monique hesitated, wondering if she should tell Doreen about the segment on *America's Most Wanted*. She decided against it, at least for now. She seemed to be the only one in the family hell-bent on finding her mother's murderer, while everyone else wanted to forget the whole ugly matter. It didn't make it an easy subject to talk about. "The police may need to speak to you."

"Of course. I'll help out any way I can. I'm not sure what good it will do, though. I didn't know anything then."

An image of her mother, bleeding on the floor, hit Monique with full force. She cringed as she suddenly fought back tears.

Instantly, Doreen wrapped an arm around her shoulder. "Monique." A little sigh escaped her. "I know I've told you this before. Somehow, you have to find a way to move on. What if they never find your mother's killer? What are you going to do? You can't let it eat away at you like this forever."

"I wish that was an option," Monique replied. "But it isn't. Every time I think I may be over it, something happens to remind me that I'm not. Sometimes it's a certain look a photographer will give me when he's photographing me, and I wonder if it was some sick pig who killed my mother because he fantasized about her in ways he shouldn't have. Or sometimes I'll be watching the news and I'll hear about a woman who's been murdered, and I'll see my mother's face."

Doreen hugged Monique harder. "You've never sought counseling in all this."

"Counseling isn't going to help."

"You should try it."

"Doreen, don't push this issue."

"Okay."

Monique stepped out of her cousin's embrace and walked toward another rack of clothing. She fingered one of the floral skirts. It was similar to a skirt she remembered her mother wearing one summer before she died. Which made Monique think of the fact that today was a gorgeous summer day. Fleetingly Monique wondered when the last time was that she'd taken time to enjoy such a day.

Not in sixteen years.

The summer reminded her of the cottage in Barrie.

And the cottage in Barrie reminded her of her mother's murder.

"The police will want to talk to Daniel, too. And probably your mother."

"We'll all do what we can."

"How often do you talk to your father?" Monique's uncle Richard had divorced Aunt Sophie around the time her father had moved to Florida, and he now lived in Ohio.

"We talk at least once a month."

"Well, if he can make himself available, that'd be great." Monique paused. "Maybe there's a clue right under our noses that we've been missing all this time."

"Maybe," Doreen said, but the word sounded placating.

"There's something else," Monique began, deciding to share everything with her cousin. "Because Mom was a high-profile model, they're going to run the story on *America's Most Wanted.*"

"Well, that's good."

Monique was surprised that Doreen didn't voice any dissent, but then, Doreen knew how pointless that would be. Anyone who knew Monique knew that she wouldn't rest until her mother's killer was found. "Hopefully, if anyone saw or heard something strange back then, it will click if they see a show about the murder." Softly, she added, "And my mother can finally have justice."

Doreen gave a grim nod. Monique knew she didn't understand her obsession with finding her mother's killer sixteen years after the fact, and she couldn't blame her. It hadn't been Doreen who'd walked into a bedroom to find her mother lying in a pool of blood. It hadn't been Doreen who'd felt so utterly helpless as she'd watched her mother's life slip away. It wasn't she who was haunted by those images even now.

Perhaps if Monique hadn't walked in and found her mother dying, this wouldn't be as bad for her. But her mother had begged Monique for her help and she hadn't been able to help her. It was something that haunted her to this day.

As if Doreen read her thoughts, she said, "There was nothing you could do, Monique."

"Maybe not then," Monique quickly replied. "But now. There's something I can do now. I can find my mother's murderer and let him face justice."

Khamil was in the checkout line at the grocery store when a magazine caught his eye. He did a double take, thinking the woman on the cover looked an awful lot like Mary.

Good Lord, it *was* Mary! Stopping, he grabbed the magazine.

"Sir?" the woman behind him asked. "Are you in the line?"

"Yes," Khamil mumbled in reply, slightly irritated with this woman's impatience. He stepped back into the line, taking the magazine with him.

No doubt about it, it was Mary all right. He'd recognize those sexy lips and beautiful brown eyes anywhere. Her eyes were staring at him, seeming to say, "Sucker!"

So she was a model. Khamil thought back to the night of the Spring Fling and grimaced. He remembered hearing that some professional models had helped organize the event, but he hadn't figured she'd been one of them. He'd met a couple of them, so why not her?

It made sense, thinking back. She was stunning. Of course she could be a model. Yet Khamil had come on to her from the position of a celebrity speaking to someone who might have admired him that night.

Man, he was a fool!

"Is that everything, sir?" the cashier asked.

"Oh. Yes," Khamil answered.

"And the magazine?"

Khamil dropped the magazine onto the conveyer belt. "Yes. I'm taking this, too."

And hopefully he'd learn more about Mary, or whatever her true name was.

So much for that idea. The magazine didn't give Khamil any clue as to who Mary really was. She'd simply graced its cover.

He knew who would have an answer. Jeremy Leeming, another lawyer at his firm, who'd also been one of the models that night, knew one of the professional female models. In fact, it had been that model who'd solicited the men of their firm to perform that night. Jeremy was sure to have some answers.

Minutes later, Khamil had Jeremy on the line. He briefly explained all that had happened, how he now realized Mary was in fact a model.

Jeremy chuckled after hearing Khamil's story.

"All right, I know," Khamil said. "But how was I to know she was one of the models?"

"You're supposed to be smart, man," Jeremy jeered playfully.

"Even I have my moments. The point is, I want to find her."

"I can call Vicky. She'll know who she is."

"Let me know the moment you find anything out."

"Will do."

* * *

Monique almost choked on her glass of wine when she saw Khamil Jordan enter the restaurant. "Oh, no," she mumbled.

"What?" Vicky asked.

Monique frowned, then tried to shield her face with a hand. "That lawyer. One of the models from the Spring Fling charity event. He just came in."

"Oooh, the hot one," Vicky chimed.

"You can say that again," Janine, one of the other models in their group of four, commented, then whistled softly.

Monique splayed her fingers over her eye, allowing herself an avenue to see Khamil. "Oh, my God. What's he doing? Is he coming this way?"

"Sorry, Monique," Vicky said. "I forgot to tell you. Jeremy called me a couple days ago and said one of his colleagues was trying to get a hold of you."

"*You* sent him here?"

"I didn't think you wouldn't want to talk to him!" Vicky protested. "Besides, what could it hurt to meet him in a public place? Then you can figure out if you're interested in him or not."

"I already met him in a public place a couple weeks ago and I *wasn't* interested."

"Girl," began Renee, the fourth model in their group tonight, "don't tell me you're still hung up on Raymond. And if you are, this man can certainly help you forget that louse. Mmm. If he isn't the hottest brother I've seen in a long time . . ."

There was no use hiding. Khamil had seen her. Monique let her hand drop from her face and tried as casually as possible to reach for her wineglass. Though she kept her eyes straight ahead, she couldn't help checking out Khamil in her peripheral vision.

He did look fine. Dressed in a slick black suit, he looked as if he had stepped off the cover of *GQ* magazine. Indeed, many wealthy and high-profile people frequented this restaurant, so Khamil wasn't overdressed, but he certainly stood out among the crowd.

"Monique Savard." Khamil's voice was cool, yet his smile didn't quite reach his eyes.

"Hello."

His eyes did a slow perusal of her body, leaving her feeling hot—and exposed. "So," he began after what seemed like hours, "do you have a moment?"

"Not really."

"Let me rephrase the question. I'd like to speak with you. Alone. Now." He smiled to soften his demand.

There was something commanding about him, something mesmerizing, something that made it hard to tell him no. Monique drew her eyes away from him and faced her friends. "If you'll excuse me for a moment."

Vicky raised one perfectly sculpted eyebrow.

Monique gave her a cool look, a look that said she shouldn't make anything of this meeting. Then she pushed her chair back and stood.

Before she knew it, Khamil had her by the elbow and was leading her to the front of the restaurant.

"I agreed to talk to you, not to leave with you!"

"Relax," Khamil said, his voice as smooth as warm chocolate. "I just want a bit of privacy, *Mary.*"

Monique's face grew warm with embarrassment. Okay, so she'd been childish giving him a false name and number, but he'd been so arrogant and full of himself, he'd been asking for it.

When Khamil had her in the entranceway of the

restaurant, he spoke. "If you didn't want me to call you, why didn't you just say so?"

Monique shrugged nonchalantly, not willing to admit she'd been childish. "You didn't seem like you'd believe it if I told you I wasn't interested."

"Hmm." Khamil studied her, trying to figure her out. And he wondered why he had actually come here. Yeah, she was attractive, but if she had lied to him about her number, then she clearly wasn't interested.

But there was something intriguing about her, he realized. Something that made him want to see her again. Coming to see her today had been like the second stage in a game, and he couldn't stop himself if he tried.

Monique stiffened her spine and crossed her arms over her chest. "Hmm what?"

Khamil gave a slight shrug. "I find you fascinating, that's all."

"Well," Monique said, as though his words didn't affect her in the least. "That's nice, but I'm sure that's not the reason you came here tonight . . ." Her voice trailed off as she almost said, "looking so good." She gave a tight smile. "Don't keep her waiting on my account."

"What?" Khamil asked, caught off guard.

But before Monique could give him an answer, she hurried back into the restaurant. A grin played on his lips as he watched her go. She didn't return to the table where she'd been sitting, as he'd anticipated, instead heading to the back of the establishment and the rest rooms.

Khamil's grin widened.

It was time for round two.

Four

Monique gasped and threw a hand to her chest when she stepped out of the bathroom door and saw Khamil standing directly in her path.

He merely smiled at her startled outburst.

Quickly recovering, Monique glared at him. "Excuse me," she said, moving to step past him.

Khamil stepped to the left, blocking her path with his muscular body. "Oh, I'm sorry," he mocked. "I didn't realize you were going to walk that way."

Monique flashed him a sarcastic smile. "Really?"

"Honest mistake."

"Fine." Monique stepped to the right, and once again, Khamil stepped with her, blocking her path.

"Oops," he said, giving Monique a boyish look.

Monique was unimpressed. "There are laws against stalking in this state."

Khamil threw his head back and laughed. "Stalking?"

"What would you call it?" Monique challenged.

"I'm merely trying to get to know you," Khamil answered frankly. "And I'll do whatever it takes."

Something stirred within Monique, but she ignored the feeling. "Didn't you get the hint when I gave you a fake name and number?"

Khamil raised an eyebrow. "Maybe you're just playing hard to get."

"You're too much," Monique said, shaking her head with chagrin. "Now please, let me pass." Once again, Monique tried to step past Khamil.

Again, he blocked her path. As Monique's dark brown eyes shot fire at him, Khamil quickly said, "All right. Maybe that was out of line."

"Yes, it was."

He stared at her a moment longer, wondering if he'd ever be able to crack the layer of ice around her. "I don't know how," he said softly, "but we've gotten off on the wrong foot."

"We haven't gotten off on *any* foot, Mr. Jordan."

"Ouch." But Khamil gave her another of his charming smiles, one that had always worked to ease tension with the opposite sex in the past.

Monique, however, seemed unaffected.

"And please," Khamil continued, wanting to keep the conversation going despite the chilly reception, "call me Khamil."

"Khamil, I have friends waiting for me."

Khamil's gaze followed a woman who brushed by him en route to the bathroom.

Monique guffawed. "Have a nice day."

"Wait." Khamil grabbed Monique's arm. "That's it? You're not going to allow me the chance to get to know you?"

"I've got an idea for you. Why not wait right here. When that woman you were just ogling comes out of the bathroom, you can see how far you get with her."

"Ogling?" Khamil looked at Monique as if she were crazy. "She nearly bumped into me. I merely looked at her to make sure she had room to pass."

"Whatever.

This wasn't working. Monique was being so cold, Khamil was getting a serious case of frostbite. "I'm simply asking for a chance to get to know you. To let you see for yourself what kind of man I am."

"That's all?"

"Yes."

"Hmm."

"What?" Khamil sensed a sudden change in Monique's attitude, and when she slowly closed the distance between them, her eyes locked with his, he held his breath.

"All right." Boldly, Monique draped her arms around Khamil's shoulders, drawing his strong body to hers.

"Wh-what are you doing?" Khamil managed. One second he was cold, the next his body was on fire.

"This is what you want, isn't it?"

"I-I . . . I have no clue what you're talking about."

"Oh, come on. You see a woman you like, you pursue her in hopes of . . . well, in hopes of, you know. Sex." Monique raised a suggestive eyebrow, then slowly and deliberately, she placed a leg around Khamil's. Khamil was powerless to do anything except stand there, powerless as she dragged her leg upward along his, stopping only when she reached his thigh.

Monique held Khamil's gaze, her dark eyes narrowed seductively. Khamil couldn't help it; his body reacted, instantly giving him a hard-on.

"Hmm?" Monique prompted. "Isn't sex what you want?"

"No. Yes. I mean no."

Monique cocked her head to the side and gave him a smug look. "Isn't it? I know men like you, playboys, who live for having women fawn all over them." She paused. "So, what's the matter?"

What indeed? Normally, if a woman was offering Khamil what Monique was, he'd jump at the opportunity to bed her and walk away. Yet he felt flustered now. And while Monique had her arms around his neck, his arms still rested at his sides—definitely not like him!

And it wasn't simply where they were. It was not knowing how to accurately read Monique.

A slow smile formed on Monique's lips.

Khamil blew out a frustrated breath, then untangled himself from Monique's body. "No, that's not what I want."

"Really?" Monique sounded shocked.

Khamil looked away as he spoke. "Yes, really."

"Good." Monique straightened her clothes. "Because you're not going to get it. At least not from me. I'm not like other women, in case you haven't figured it out."

Khamil was too stunned to say a word.

Suddenly, Monique felt bad. She had no clue what possessed her to so brazenly come on to Khamil, only to let him down. Maybe because she'd met one too many guys like him over the years, especially since establishing herself as one of New York's hottest fashion models. But the bewildered look on Khamil's face, as well as the hint of embarrassment in his eyes, had her regretting what she'd just done.

For the first time, Monique sensed a nice side to Khamil Jordan. Her shoulders drooped, the fight going out of her. "Khamil, I don't want to offend you, but I'm just not interested. You're not my type."

Khamil was still trying to make sense of whatever game Monique was playing, and at Monique's last statement, he felt a painful little jolt in his chest. He didn't move or say a word, merely stared down at Monique, waiting for her to crack a smile—anything to let him know she was joking. But he received merely an unwavering, albeit somewhat contrite, look.

"I see," Khamil said tightly. He still didn't understand her, but now at least he'd gotten the point. She wasn't interested.

"Now, I really do have to get back to my friends."

Khamil gave a grim nod, then watched Monique turn around. He watched her stop midpivot, watched her body freeze. Instantly, she spun back around. She hesitated only a second before marching toward him.

"Kiss me."

"What?"

Monique threw her arms around Khamil's shoulders. "Just—" Monique stopped herself short as she tipped on her toes and locked lips with his.

"Wait a . . ." Khamil mumbled against her velvety soft lips, but when Monique softly moaned and pressed her body closer to his, Khamil couldn't help reacting. He wrapped his arms around her, enjoying the feel of her curvaceous body in his arms. And when Monique parted her lips, he eagerly delved his tongue into her hot, sweet mouth.

While a moment ago he'd wondered what her game was, right now he didn't care. All he cared about was this beautiful woman, how sweet her lips tasted, how the delicate scent of her perfume was driving him wild. He wanted her, and he had the erection to prove it.

And as suddenly as it began, it ended.

Monique stepped away from Khamil and asked, "Is he still there?"

Khamil stared down at her as if she'd grown horns. "What on earth—"

"There was a guy behind me a moment ago."

Monique spoke somewhat breathlessly, and knew she'd be lying to herself if she said it was because she'd seen Raymond unexpectedly. She hadn't expected Khamil to react to the kiss the way he had; she hadn't expected her own body to thrum with excitement.

She pushed the disturbing thought from her mind as she assessed Khamil's perplexed look. She may as well have been speaking Russian, considering how she wasn't getting through to him.

"There was a man," she repeated, her tone low. "African-American, around six feet tall, slim build. He was standing behind me a moment ago. Is he still there?"

A small scowl marred Khamil's handsome features as he looked past Monique. "I don't see anyone there now."

Monique's shoulders sagged with relief. "Good." She glanced over her shoulder to verify that Khamil was correct. There was no sign of Raymond. When she faced Khamil once more, she found dark, intense eyes boring into hers. He didn't speak, which unnerved her even more.

"I'll . . . uh . . . I'm going back now," she completed, gesturing a thumb over her shoulder to indicate she planned to head back into the restaurant's dining room.

Before she could move, Khamil darted a hand out, wrapping his strong fingers around her slim wrist. "You kiss me, then you plan to walk away without another word?"

"Well, I . . . Look, there was a guy behind me, someone I didn't want to see." She gave him a sheepish look. "I'm sorry I kissed you, but it was the only thing I could think of to do at the time, so he'd get the picture that I've moved on."

Khamil urged Monique closer, and she stumbled, falling against his thick chest. Her heart rate doubled, and she slowly raised her eyes until she met his look dead-on.

"Are you saying you kissed me to prove a point to someone else?" Khamil's tone sounded almost lethal.

"Yes," Monique said feebly, instantly hating how unsure of herself she sounded. "Yes," she repeated, firmly this time, even though she did glance away as she said the word.

But she couldn't look away for long. There was something about Khamil that was strangely compelling, even though she knew men like him and hated the type.

He raised an eyebrow as she met his gaze, a challenge sparking in his eyes. "So the kiss then . . . you didn't feel a thing."

Every nerve in Monique's body was on fire, yet she replied, "That's right. I didn't feel a thing."

"And when you wrapped your body around mine, that was just to show me how much you *didn't* want me?"

"Right again."

"Liar."

The word startled Monique, not so much because of what he said, but because of the intensity with which he'd said it. Because of how he'd neared his lips to a fraction of an inch from hers when he'd spoken. Because of how badly, at that moment, Monique had wanted to kiss him again.

This was wrong, all wrong. Why was she even thinking of the possibility of kissing him again? He wasn't her type, and she most certainly didn't want to get to know him.

Monique wrestled her arm from Khamil's grasp and took a step backward. "I'm leaving."

"Can't deal with your feelings?"

"Khamil, you're not my type."

"But you're still attracted to me."

"God, you have an ego the size of Mount Everest."

"I call 'em like I see 'em."

"Well, in this case you'd better get some glasses."

"Is that right?"

"That's right," Monique agreed, then spun around on her heel. She hurried away from Khamil, away from her confusing emotions, and back to the table where she'd left her friends.

"Hey," she said, taking her seat again.

"Hey?" Vicky gave her a disapproving look. "You disappeared forever with Mr. Hottie, and all you're gonna say is *hey?*"

"There's nothing to tell, Vicky," Monique quickly replied. "Except that I saw Raymond. Oh, no," she said as she looked around and saw him at the nearby bar. "I don't think I'm up for this tonight."

"Don't let him bother you."

Monique guffawed. "Yeah, right. Someone should tell him that." Monique had no doubt that he was there because he knew he could always find her there on Thursday nights. For someone who'd seemed so nice in the beginning, he certainly was acting like an obsessed idiot.

Monique pulled her purse strap over her shoulder and stood. "I'm gonna go."

"Oh, come on," Renee pleaded. "We'll make sure he doesn't bother you."

"I'm not in the mood to hang out anymore," Monique replied succinctly, then leaned over and kissed both Vicky and Renee on the cheek, then squeezed Janine's hand as she couldn't reach her for a peck. "Talk to you later."

She heard her friends mumbling about her as she turned to leave, but couldn't make out what they were saying. Monique threw a surreptitious gaze in the direction of the bar. A wave of relief passed over her when she saw that Raymond was no longer there. In fact, she didn't see him anywhere. Still, she hastily made her way through the populated restaurant, heading to the front door.

"Monique."

She halted at the sound of Khamil's voice, as though his voice alone had the power to make her do anything he wanted.

"Monique," he repeated.

Slowly, she turned. Seeing him again was like seeing him for the first time; he literally took her breath away. Yes, he was fine. Too bad he was the type of brother who thought his good looks meant he was some type of god.

"Yes."

"You're leaving?"

"Yes."

"So am I. I'll walk you out."

Monique didn't argue. And she didn't move away from Khamil's touch as he placed a hand on her back and guided her through the restaurant. As much as she told herself she didn't like him, there was something strangely comforting about his presence and his touch, especially right now when she was worried about where Raymond was.

Outside, Khamil said, "Where do you live?"

Monique's eyes widened with alarm.

"I just meant, will you be okay getting home?"

"Oh. Yeah, I'll be fine. I live near Central Park. I'll catch a cab."

Khamil nodded, then looked at her, as though he wanted to say something else. Monique waited. When he didn't say anything, she spoke. "All right, then. Get home safe."

Monique turned before Khamil had the chance to say anything else. She hailed an oncoming cab, and within seconds she was inside, staring back at Khamil as the cab merged into traffic.

Five

Monique screamed when she stepped into her penthouse and turned on the light switch in the foyer.

"Raymond!" she exclaimed, clutching a hand to her heart. He was standing a few feet away from her, at the entrance to the living room. Until she'd turned on the light, he'd been standing there in the dark. Clearly, he'd planned to surprise her. "What in God's name—"

"I needed to see you," he said, walking toward her.

Monique stiffened her spine. "You gave me back the key. How did you get in here?"

"I made a copy," he admitted.

Monique wondered why he hadn't used it before now. Probably because he was giving her time to come to her senses and realize that she loved him, but considering she hadn't, he was now putting on the pressure. She'd have to tell the concierge that Raymond was no longer welcome in her home.

"Baby—"

"Don't call me that."

Raymond leaned against the wall and blew out a ragged breath. "You're right, I shouldn't have come here like this, and I'm sorry. I just needed to see you, and when you wouldn't return my calls . . ."

"There's nothing left for us to say, Raymond. I'm willing to be your friend, if for no other reason than I'll probably have to work with you again, but to be quite honest, you're making that very difficult right now."

"Who's the guy?"

"What guy?"

"The guy who had his tongue down your throat," Raymond snapped.

Monique kicked off her shoes and stepped past Raymond into the living room. "I want you to leave."

Instead of heading to the door, he was right on her heel, startling Monique. "You told me you were going to take some time and see what you wanted from our relationship."

"No, *you* told me that's what I should do. I told you it was over."

"Why?"

"Raymond, you cheated on me."

"And I'm sorry. It won't happen again."

"That's right, it won't. At least not with me." Monique paused. "Look, I think what happened shows that I just don't have time in my life right now for a relationship. Neither do you."

"This is about your mother."

Monique felt a stab of pain in her chest. She regretted ever telling Raymond about her mother's murder. Every time she felt down, he blamed it on that. When she couldn't forgive his affair, he blamed it on that. When she said she needed time away from him, he blamed it on that. He seemed to think that if he could make everything better in that regard, she would be his.

"This is about us," Monique responded slowly. "We're not right for each other."

"What if I could help you solve your mother's murder, would you give me another chance?"

Monique was momentarily startled by the question. She wondered what would possess Raymond to say such a thing. She asked him exactly that.

"What if I knew something, or knew someone who did?"

"Raymond, I don't have time for games."

"I want to help you, Monique, but if I'm going to give you something, you should be willing to give me something in return—another chance with you."

"Raymond, do you know something or not?"

He didn't answer, and his eyes said he expected her to agree to his terms before he'd tell her a thing.

Monique sneered at him. "Leave, Raymond. Now."

"Fine," he said, with a nonchalant shrug of his shoulders, one that said she'd made her choice and would have to live with the consequences.

Raymond had started toward the door when Monique said, "Give me the key."

He stopped, angrily fished the key out of his pocket, then tossed it to her. It sailed past her, landing on the carpeted floor.

Monique didn't make a move for it, instead giving Raymond a lethal look that didn't match her inner trembling. She wasn't about to let him intimidate her.

Without another word, he turned.

Her body trembling from both anger and anxiety, Monique watched Raymond's slim form walk toward the door, then out of the condo. The moment he was gone, she ran to the door and bolted it shut.

Then she pressed her forehead and both palms against the door and rested there for several seconds.

What if he does know something? she asked herself.

He couldn't, she decided, heaving herself off the door. He would use anything to try and get her back, even the pain of her mother's murder. How low the man would stoop was beyond her.

If he had cared so much about her before, then why had he cheated on her? Whatever the answer, Monique knew that this situation was too messed up for her to ever be dumb enough to give Raymond another chance.

How could she, when she didn't quite trust him?

A week after sharing that kiss with Monique, Khamil couldn't stop thinking about her.

He wasn't sure if it was because she had embarrassed him royally, but Khamil Jordan wasn't used to women playing him the way Monique had.

Maybe it was pride telling him he had to see her again and get one up on her. Play her and leave her feeling hot and bothered as she had done to him. But if he were to be honest with himself, he'd have to admit that his wanting to see her again had nothing to do with wanting to prove any such thing.

He wanted simply to see her again, and to know that this time he could have an effect on her.

Though he knew that he'd had *some* type of effect on her. She was either hot or cold with him, which meant she felt something. And he had watched her watching him as the cab had driven off. If he wasn't mistaken, he'd sensed a struggle within her as she'd looked at him. If not, why hadn't she simply looked away? She was attracted to him, despite that nonsense she'd said about him not being her type.

You didn't kiss someone the way she had kissed him and then say you felt nothing unless you were lying to yourself.

The phone rang, interrupting Khamil's thoughts. He hurried to answer it. "Hello?"

"Khamil."

"Hey, Javar!" Khamil exclaimed, elated to hear the voice of his elder brother by a year. "What's up, my man?"

"Just calling to see how things are going in your part of the world."

"Oh, same-old, same-old. Busy as usual."

"Take it from me, you need to slow down. I never listened to Whitney for years when she said I needed to take on a partner or two, but now that I have, I couldn't be happier."

Whitney was Javar's wife of seven years. The first two years they'd been blissfully happy, until a tragedy had torn them apart. Whitney had been driving her car with Javar's son, J. J. —her stepson—and had gotten into an accident. Unfortunately, the accident had killed five-year-old J. J.

At first, Javar had seemed incapable of forgiving Whitney for the accident, but he'd really been so consumed with grief that he hadn't known how to deal with it. Whitney had been torn up over the whole incident herself, living with a great deal of guilt. Although the roads were wet at the time, she still blamed herself for the accident. She'd needed Javar's love and support, and he hadn't been able to give it. Ultimately, she'd left him and gone to live with an aunt in Louisiana.

Two years later, she had returned to Chicago, where Khamil and his family had grown up, to seek a divorce. And when she'd ended up in another car accident that landed her in the hospital with life-threatening injuries, Javar had realized how much he still loved her and didn't want to lose her. Khamil had always liked Whitney, from the night he and his brother had met her in a Chicago club and his brother had fallen head over heels for her. Unlike his mother and sister, who wanted Whitney out of Javar's life, he had hoped they would work out their problems.

To this day, Khamil still had trouble dealing with the reality of just how badly his mother hadn't wanted Whitney in Javar's life. His own mother had tried to kill her, but luckily Javar had gotten to Whitney in time. But the worst part was learning that his mother had sabotaged Whitney's car, which had resulted in her not being able to control it on the rain-slicked roads as she'd driven with little J. J. It was his mother's fault that his nephew had been tragically killed.

Now, she was spending the next several years in prison.

But at least Javar and Whitney had worked out their problems and were once again happy.

"Khamil?"

"Huh?" he asked, realizing his mind had drifted.

"I asked, are you too busy to see your brother? I'm coming to town next week."

A smile spread on Khamil's face. "Of course I'm not too busy for you!" He didn't see his brother, nor the rest of his family, as often as he liked these days.

"Whitney was going to come, as we have a surprise for you, but she won't be able to make it now."

"A surprise? What, you trying to set me up with one of her friends?"

"Hey, she knows better than to sic you on any of her friends."

"I resent that."

Javar chuckled. "Whatever."

"Then what kind of surprise?"

"She's pregnant again."

"All right!" Khamil couldn't help shouting. Then, he felt an odd moment of emptiness. These days, it felt as if he was living vicariously through his brother's life. Hearing this good news reminded him that he had yet to find the perfect woman, the one he would settle down and start a family with.

Once again, Monique popped into his mind, but Khamil did his best to block her out. She was definitely not wife material. Not that she wasn't beautiful enough, but any woman he would marry would have to *like* him first.

"Yeah, Whitney's almost six months along, but recently started cramping. We were worried she was going into premature labor, but she wasn't."

"Oh, no."

"No, everything's fine. The doctor just said she ought to take it easy, so she's gonna skip this trip."

"Wait a minute . . . did you say *six* months?"

"Uh-huh."

"And you're just telling me *now*?"

"Like I said, Whitney wanted to surprise you, but now that she can't . . ." Javar's voice trailed off.

"How are Reanna and Marcus?"

"Great." Javar paused. "Nothing will ever take the place of J. J., but I feel like I've been given a second chance to do things right. With J. J., I didn't make time to do things with him the way a father should, because I was always too concerned about providing for my family. Then, I lost him and couldn't make up for the years of misspent energy. Now, I'm definitely not making that mistake, and I'm having a blast being a husband and father."

A smile touched Khamil's lips. "I'm glad to hear it, bro. You deserve it."

"My next wish is to see you settle down," Javar said, a smile in his voice.

"When—"

"—the right woman comes along, I'll be more than happy to settle down," Javar finished for Khamil, indicating just how many times he'd heard him say that.

Khamil chuckled. "Mock me all you want, it's the truth."

"I'll believe it when I see it."

Having spoken to his brother, Khamil couldn't concentrate on work. He was excited for Javar and Whitney, but once again, that empty feeling was back.

He wasn't exactly sure why that empty feeling had him thinking of Monique, but he did know that he needed to see her. According to his colleague, Monique and her model friends always went to Angel's on Thursday nights, and since it was Thursday . . .

He hadn't eaten yet, and the food was good there. He liked the ambience.

And hey, it was a free country.

Within the hour, Khamil was showered, dressed, and walking through the door of Angel's.

The host immediately greeted him. "Table for one?"

"I'm meeting someone," Khamil replied, looking past the young man into the restaurant. He glanced in the direction of the table where he'd found Monique the first time. Seeing Vicky, he smiled.

But the smile slowly disappeared as he headed toward the table and didn't see Monique. He felt a sense of disappointment, something he wasn't used to feeling. An instant later, he realized she was most likely in the bathroom, and joy lifted his heart once again.

Vicky gave him a bright smile as she looked up and saw him. "Khamil!"

She jumped out of her seat and wrapped him in a hug. The way she greeted him, you'd think she'd known him for years.

Khamil politely moved back, placing a chaste kiss on Vicky's cheek. He recognized her actions for what they were—an advance. She was letting him know in no uncertain terms that she wanted him. He was flattered, but also a little annoyed. Vicky was Monique's friend, and had to know that he was interested in her. Did Vicky's advances mean that Monique had told Vicky she had no interest in Khamil whatsoever, and that he was up for grabs?

"Where's Monique?" he asked.

Vicky's smile flattened. "Oh, Monique couldn't make it tonight."

"Really?" The disappointment was back, like a kick in the gut.

"Yeah, she had something to do. Personal business," she added with a little shrug.

"Hmm." Khamil was tempted to ask exactly how personal her business was, but didn't. He didn't have a right. Just as he didn't have a right to feel a pang of jealousy, yet he did. The way Vicky spoke made it sound as if Monique was out with a man. Was it the guy she'd tried to avoid when she had kissed him here in this restaurant, just last week?

"Feel free to join us, if you like."

Vicky's voice interrupted Khamil's thoughts. He looked down at the two other women at the table, knowing that it would be any man's fantasy to spend the evening with three gorgeous models, yet he said, "No, thanks. I just came by to see Monique. I . . . I had to give her something."

"I can give it to her, if you like," Vicky offered.

Khamil shook his head. "Naw, that's okay. I'd rather give it to her when I see her." Of course, he was lying, and wouldn't be able to produce anything worthy of passing along to Monique if his life depended on it. But Vicky didn't need to know that. "Just tell her I was looking for her, if she happens to come in."

"Sure," Vicky said.

Khamil gave a smile and nod to the other women at the table, who looked up at him with sly grins. A faint voice in his head asked if he was nuts to walk away from these women.

No, he wasn't nuts. Monique was the one he was interested in, and he didn't want to confuse any of them, especially Vicky, by spending time with them if Monique wasn't around.

Still, as Khamil headed for the front door of the restaurant, he wondered when he had changed so drastically.

Six

When Monique finally arrived home, she went straight to her bedroom and collapsed on her king-size bed, letting out a loud moan as she did. The day's events had drained her. She'd done a catalogue shoot for lingerie and swimwear, which made for a long day as it was, but the day had been even longer as she'd been accompanied by a camera crew from *America's Most Wanted* on the shoot. The camera crew had captured film of her in her work environment for the show, and after that she'd done an interview about her mother's murder.

She was pleased with how it all went, even though the subject of her mother's murder had naturally brought her down. Hopefully, the airing of this story on national television would reach someone who knew something about the case, enabling the killer to be caught once and for all.

Monique rolled onto her back, resting her forearm across her forehead. She contemplated calling her father. She hadn't talked to him about the fact that the police were reopening her mother's murder investigation.

Part of her was afraid. She knew, based on past experience when dealing with her father about this subject, that he wouldn't be happy about it. That was the one thing that gave her pause on those very few occasions that she allowed herself to wonder if her father could possibly have had anything to do with her mother's death. But as quickly as that disturbing thought came into her mind, it fled. She suspected that her father's seeming indifference to whether or not her mother's killer was ever brought to justice had to do with the fact that he didn't trust the police to be able to do so.

After all, they had wasted two years trying to pin the crime on him. With only circumstantial evidence, they'd ultimately been unable to prove her father guilty of anything other than being perhaps a little intimidated by his wife's success.

She had deliberately avoided calling her father about this issue, but she would have to tell him what was happening before the show aired.

Sitting up, Monique stretched, then reached for the phone on her night table. She was caught off guard when she realized there was no dial tone.

"Hello . . ." a voice on the other line said.

"Vicky?" Monique asked.

"Yep."

"Oh. The phone didn't ring." She sat up. "What's up?"

"Nothing much. I was calling to see how things went today."

"Very well, I think," Monique responded. "I got to meet John Walsh," she added, her tone upbeat.

"Ah, so you did."

"Yep. He's really a sweetheart, made me feel very comfortable right from the beginning. It's obvious he really cares about the victims of crime and their families."

"I never watch the show."

"I do." Monique paused. "You never know, psychos may be walking among us, living next door, working with us." Her tone was lighthearted, but she was completely serious. And she was hoping that other people like her, people interested in justice, would watch the show and remember that muggy summer night sixteen years ago in Barrie.

"So what did you talk about?" Vicky asked. "For the interview, that is."

"He asked me how my mother's murder had affected my life—that sort of thing. Then we spoke about the fact that my mother had been harassed by a stalker before her death, and given that fact, why had I decided to follow in her career path." It was the very same question her father had asked her. "I told him I'd do anything to find my mother's killer."

"Hmm," was all Vicky said.

"They'll be heading to Canada next to interview the detectives working on this case. In fact, the entire episode is going to focus on Canadian crimes."

"And when will it air?"

"Next week." Monique paused, then asked, "How was it tonight?"

"The usual," Vicky replied casually. Then, "Oh, guess who dropped by?"

Monique's stomach instantly fluttered, though she didn't know why. "Who?" she asked, though she had a sneaking suspicion who Vicky was talking about.

"Khamil," her friend practically sang.

"Khamil?" Monique's voice was barely above a whisper as the butterflies went wild in her stomach.

"Mmm-hmm. He came by tonight."

Vicky had a flair for the dramatic, often making Monique pull information out of her. As much as Monique wanted to pretend that Khamil's showing up was of no interest to her, that was a lie. "So," she began after a moment. "What did he want?"

"He came by to hang out."

"Oh." Monique was disappointed. "So he stayed a while."

"A little while."

Well, there went any fantasy that he may have shown up to see her. Which, to Monique's chagrin, she realized mattered. That fact irked her, because she didn't want to give Khamil even a second thought.

"Tell me something," Vicky began. "Do you . . . well, are you interested in Khamil?"

"Why?" Monique asked quickly. Too late, she realized she may have sounded a tad defensive. But she couldn't help wondering why it should matter to Vicky if she was or wasn't interested in Khamil.

"I'm just wondering," Vicky replied casually. "He *is* fine. And . . ." Vicky's voice trailed off. "Well, he said he had something for you, so I was wondering if you're holding out on me or something."

"He had something for me?" Monique couldn't hide her shock. "What?"

"He didn't say. He just said he'd give it to you another time."

"Really?" Monique's mind worked overtime, trying to figure out exactly what Khamil could have had for her. And she also tried to figure out if Vicky was interested in making a play for Khamil. She wasn't sure.

"Really."

"I have no idea what it could be," Monique admitted. "But I'll call him. Thanks."

"So you have his number."

"Yeah, I do." Monique didn't offer any more explanation than that. "Anyway, hon, I'm exhausted, and I have to call my father."

"And Khamil." Vicky giggled. "Listen, girl, I want all the details, you hear?"

Monique gave a little chuckle. "Sure. Talk to you later."

"Bye."

When Monique hung up, she stared at the phone, thinking she should call her father. But her curiosity over Khamil's visit got the better of her, and she decided to call him.

The card he'd given her with his number on it was in her wallet, so Monique reached for her purse on the floor beside her bed, withdrew the wallet, then searched for Khamil's card. Once she found it, her heart did an erratic pitter-patter in her chest.

Why was she so nervous? She was an adult. She could call him and be professional. Who knew what he had to give her?

Before she lost her courage, she punched in the digits to his home number.

He answered after the first ring. "Hello?"

Monique paused, then sucked in a nervous breath. She didn't realize she'd paused too long until Khamil spoke one more time.

"Uh, hi. Khamil?"

"Yes?"

"Hi." Monique forced a smile into her voice. "This is Monique Savard."

"Monique. To what do I owe this honor?"

"I heard you were at Angel's today."

"Yes, I was."

Monique waited, but Khamil didn't offer any further explanation. Maybe he hadn't stopped by to see her. Maybe he'd stopped by to see Vicky, and that's why Vicky had called to ask her about the nature of her relationship with Khamil.

"I was hoping to see you," Khamil said after a moment.

Monique felt a strange tingling in her arms, chest,

and stomach. Excitement, she realized. Lord help her, she couldn't believe she was actually excited to hear that Khamil *had* gone to the restaurant to see her.

How long could she lie to herself and say she wasn't the least bit interested in Khamil? It was obvious. The mere sound of his deep, seductive voice made her head spin. And she had to admit she'd been insecure that he wasn't interested, and perhaps interested in Vicky, until he'd said the words she'd wanted to hear.

Her old insecurities from her relationship with Raymond had reared. Just because Raymond had played her didn't mean Khamil would.

"Monique?"

"Sorry," she quickly said, realizing she'd been lost in her own thoughts.

"It's probably none of my business, but Vicky said you had personal business to attend to . . ." Khamil's voice trailed.

"Yeah."

There was a pause; then Khamil asked, "Anything you want to talk about?"

"Not really."

"Oh." Disappointment stabbed him, like a knife in the heart. Which surprised him. It was a feeling he hadn't experienced in ages, since Dawn. Almost as if he were . . . jealous.

Yeah, he was jealous. Why else would Monique not want to say anything about what she'd done, unless that *personal* business had to do with a man?

Maybe Khamil was blowing the situation out of proportion, because in reality, she didn't owe him any explanation about what she did and didn't do in her life. Still, he couldn't shake the uneasy feeling in his gut.

"Vicky said you had something for me," Monique said after what seemed like ages.

"Uh . . ." Khamil didn't know what to say. Of course, he hadn't had a thing for Monique. That had simply been an excuse to drop by. Why couldn't he simply tell her that he wanted to take her out to dinner sometime?

Because he'd already told her he was interested, and she'd rebuffed him in a grand way.

But that kiss . . .

Meant to prove a point to some other guy. The last thing he had time for was a woman who was hung up on someone else.

"I was in the area and I had tickets for the theater tonight," Khamil lied. "So I figured I'd ask you. No big deal."

"I see," Monique said, but she didn't. Once again, she was feeling insecure. Khamil's tone now was aloof, and she wasn't sure if he was actually interested or not. "You could have asked Vicky."

"I would have, but I decided not to bother going. It was a spur-of-the-moment decision to even go, since I'm so busy with work and rarely take any time for myself. So, since you weren't there . . . Like I said, no big deal."

A lump of emotion formed in Monique's throat. Why she'd even bothered to allow herself the small fantasy that Khamil was interested in her beyond a physical attraction, she didn't know.

She remembered this feeling of disappointment well. It was further proof that she didn't have time in her life for a man and all the ups and downs that came with having one.

"Well," she announced, "I just figured I'd call to see what you wanted. Now I know." Pause. "I'll let you go."

Khamil didn't say anything right away, making Monique wonder if he wanted to say something else. *Silly,* she chided herself. Khamil was the kind of man who said what was on his mind. As she'd suspected, he'd been interested initially, but a player like him had already moved on to a new flavor.

"Okay, then," Khamil said. "Good night."

"Good night," Monique replied in a clipped tone. Then she quickly hung up, telling herself over and over that Khamil's lack of interest in her didn't matter.

Seven

"America's Most Wanted? What the hell were you thinking?"

"Calm down, Daniel," Monique said. She looked from him to his sister, then to her aunt. She was at their Bronx home this evening for dinner.

"I don't see how this is going to help at all," Daniel continued. "You're a high-profile model. The only response you'll get is from nutcases who want attention, and they'll give the police all sorts of bogus leads."

Monique loved her cousin, but for as long as she'd known him, he'd always been a brooding man, one to see the negative before ever seeing the positive.

"He could be right," Doreen said.

"I don't think so," Monique countered. "The police are well trained in sifting through legitimate leads and bogus ones." She looked at Daniel, Doreen, and her aunt Sophie in turn. "Besides, this is great exposure. Yes, I'm a successful model, but that's the reason they want to feature this story. Because my mother was a successful model, murdered in her prime, and now I'm continuing her legacy. That's the kind of thing that interests people."

Aunt Sophie said, "A couple years ago, when that magazine featured your story, nothing came of that."

"Who knows who read that magazine? This show will reach a much broader audience—across the border as well where the crime actually happened. I have to hope someone who knows something will be watching the show when it airs."

"Your mother has been dead for sixteen years," Daniel suddenly said. "Yes, I'm sorry it happened, I'm sorry her killer was never brought to justice. But what good is it going to do to reopen the investigation now?"

Monique looked at her cousin point-blank, disappointed. "For one thing, it wasn't my decision to reopen the case. The police chose to do that. But I'm damn glad they're doing it, because my mother's killer has gone without justice for way too long." Again, she glanced at each of her relatives. "I thought you'd all understand that."

"I think," Aunt Sophie began, "Daniel is simply trying to say that this will all bring so much pain with it . . . and there's been enough pain. Sometimes, we just don't get the closure we want and need. But life has to go on."

"And if the opportunity arises for another chance to catch my mother's killer, why shouldn't I be glad?"

Aunt Sophie merely glanced at her food, then shrugged. No one was eating much of their dinner. "What does your father say?" she asked after a moment.

"I haven't told him yet," Monique confessed.

"Don't you think he should have a say in all this?" Daniel challenged.

"I'm not exactly sure why you're so against this, Daniel." Monique's tone was brusque, but she was most definitely annoyed now. "I'm the one who's going to be in the spotlight, if anything. The most the police will ask of you is to give them your account of what happened that night. How's that going to hurt you?"

"God," Daniel snapped, then pushed his chair back. "Why can't you just leave well enough alone?" He glared at her for a brief second before storming from the dining room.

Monique stared after him, both baffled and hurt.

Doreen gave a little shrug. "Don't mind him, Monique. He's got other things on his mind. He's really stressed at work. And he and Charlene are having problems—again."

"Mmm-hmm," Monique said, though Doreen's explanation for her brother's rude behavior didn't make her feel any better. She looked down at her plate, her piece of lasagna hardly eaten. No longer hungry, she pushed the plate away.

"Well, like I told you before, the show's gonna air tonight," Monique said. "I'm sorry I didn't tell you before now, but please understand, this is something I had to do." She'd left a message for her father about the show, but he hadn't gotten back to her. She hoped he understood, too. Sometimes, it seemed she was the only one in her family who cared about getting justice in this case.

"And let's pray that this time," Monique added, "there are some results."

"Not tonight," Khamil told Macy.

"Oh." He could hear a frown in Macy's voice. "Maybe tomorrow, then?"

"Maybe," Khamil replied. He already had the remote in his hands and was flipping through the television stations until he got to the one he wanted.

"Listen, Macy, you know I'm gonna have to call you back. It's almost nine o'clock."

"Ah, that's right." Macy *tsk*ed. "You and that show."

"Yeah, me and that show. It's the one show I must see every week, as you know. So, I'll talk to you later, okay?"

Macy replied by making a frustrated sound and hanging up. *Oh well,* Khamil thought as he replaced the receiver. He didn't care. She must have thought he wouldn't reject her for a TV show, but such was life. Besides, he wasn't interested in hanging out tonight, plain and simple, and definitely not with Macy. Like the other women who'd come into his life, she had been fun for a while, but there was nothing special about her, and he didn't want to lead her on by spending more time with her if he wasn't truly interested.

He had friends who would continue to see women for companionship and sex, all the while knowing they had no plans for a future with them. Those same friends would come to Khamil for advice when the particular woman they were seeing gave them stress about wanting to settle down. In the end, there was unnecessary heartache, all of which could have been prevented if the men had just been open and honest about their feelings, and stopped seeing whatever woman when he realized there wasn't a future in the relationship.

Khamil found the station he was looking for, then settled into his sofa to prepare for the beginning of the show. *America's Most Wanted* was must-see TV for him, and he didn't like to miss it unless there was some type of emergency.

It wasn't morbid fascination with crime; in fact, Khamil always hoped he'd be able to recognize someone wanted for a heinous crime. He was a firm believer in right and wrong, at least where the law was concerned. If you do the crime, you do the time, was his favorite motto, and no one could accuse him of playing favorites. Three years ago, his mother had been convicted of attempted murder and involuntary manslaughter, and while he loved her, he knew she had to face justice the same way anyone else should. He also believed in forgiveness, and knew that people could change—only if they wanted to. Unfortunately, his mother continued to justify her actions—attempted murder as a way to protect her son from a woman she believed was a gold digger. His sister-in-law, Whitney, was so far from the calculating manipulative user his mother had made her out to be, and Khamil hoped one day his mother would finally see that.

Khamil watched the show, both horrified by the scope of the crimes and intrigued by just what made some people choose that path. Perhaps he was still trying to find answers for his mother's own bizarre behavior. While he knew his mother had been worried about Javar being taken advantage of, it was one thing to be a concerned parent and quite another to take the step she had.

"*Up next,*" the host said, "*a young girl finds her dying mother. It was too late for her to help her mother then, but maybe we can help her daughter get justice now.*"

And then, to Khamil's utter shock, he saw Monique's face appear on the screen.

"*It's a nightmare that haunts me every day,*" Monique said.

Then the show went to a commercial.

Khamil had been about to get up and get a soft drink, but now he remained rooted to the spot on his leather sofa, waiting for the commercials to end.

Had he been imagining things, or had that actually been Monique Savard on the television?

It seemed like ages before the show returned, and as John Walsh began to speak about a young girl whose mother had been murdered sixteen years ago, Khamil's heart beat double time. The still pictures that flashed across the screen were of a woman who *had* to be Monique's mother. She looked so much like her, the two could pass for twins.

"But Julia Savard's career ended in the early morning hours of July 17, 1985, when someone brutally stabbed this successful model, mother, and wife, leaving her to die." The pictures changed from beautiful shots of Julia Savard to quick pictures of a body lying on a bedroom floor, accompanied by sinister-sounding music. *"Hearing her mother's faint cries, Monique Savard rushed into her mother's bedroom and found her bleeding from multiple stab wounds."*

The scene went to a shot of Monique sitting on a chair, behind which were pictures of her mother and of her, in casual as well as professional poses. *"I still remember thinking that I must have been dreaming,"* Monique said. *"I remember walking into my mother's room and thinking I must have been having a nightmare. Well, it was a nightmare. It's a nightmare that haunts me every day."* Monique dabbed at her eyes, wiping a stray tear that had fallen. *"I keep wondering what would have happened if I'd gotten to my mother a moment sooner. Would she still be alive?"* Monique lowered her head as her voice cracked.

"Monique was young at the time of the murder, only fourteen years old," John Walsh said. *"She remembers hearing a car squealing off in the night, but as she hurried to call 911, she never managed to look outside.*

"Now, Monique has followed in the footsteps of her mother, and is a successful model in New York." The back-

ground music was now upbeat, as Monique was portrayed during some type of photo shoot.

"She knows her mother was stalked by an obsessed fan, but that doesn't scare her."

"I want to keep my mother's legacy alive," Monique said, the camera once again showing her sitting on a chair. *"I can't let the person who snuffed out her life snuff out her spirit. By doing what I'm doing, I'm honoring my mother. And if there's an element of danger, that doesn't scare me. All I care about is finding my mother's killer."*

The screen went back to John Walsh, who was standing on a dark street somewhere in the city of Toronto. *"Monique and her family have had no answers in sixteen years, and they need them. Julia's husband, Lucas Savard, was initially considered a suspect in this heinous crime, but no charges were officially filed against him. It's been sixteen years too long that a killer has been able to walk the streets, unpunished. The Savard family will only have closure when Julia's killer is brought to justice.*

"There aren't a lot of clues in this case, but we've solved tougher cases than this one, and I know someone out there knows something. Don't be afraid to make that call. Now, on to our next case . . ."

Khamil let out a long swoosh of air once the segment featuring Monique was over, unaware that he'd even been holding his breath. Whoa, whoa, whoa! Monique Savard's mother had been murdered?

A million thoughts were going through Khamil's mind. How had he not known? That wasn't a rational thought, of course, because how *could* he have known? He and Monique weren't friends; in fact, they had barely spoken. It certainly didn't make sense that the first thing she'd say to him was, "Hi, my name's Monique. My mother was murdered sixteen years ago."

Besides shock and compassion, the other emotion

Khamil felt was a sudden and intense burst of fear. Was she okay? If a stalker had harassed her mother, one could surely harass her. And if she lived alone in New York City . . . Khamil didn't want to entertain the possibilities of how at risk she may be, given her high-profile career.

Wow. Monique's mother had been murdered. One would never tell to look at her, but then no one would know from looking at him that his mother was serving time in prison. While some people thought him shallow, namely because he was still single at thirty-eight and had had his share of women, he was far deeper than most people realized. He had the capacity to give love, the capacity to care. And he'd always empathized with victims of crime, understanding their pain and frustration in a way that even he didn't comprehend.

Now, knowing the truth about Monique's past, he felt a strange pang in his heart. Having watched Monique on the show, having seen her moved to tears as she recounted the night of her mother's murder, he couldn't help but feel pain on her behalf.

And, Lord help him, he felt like an inconsiderate fool.

She'd accused him of being a stalker, something he had laughed off at the time because he'd assumed she was simply playing hard to get, or at worst, giving him the cold shoulder. Now he knew her words had a deeper meaning. Maybe he *had* scared her by coming on too strong. And even if he hadn't actually scared her, he'd no doubt reminded her of what had happened to her mother.

Khamil slapped a palm against his forehead. What should he do? Apologize to her? He hadn't meant any harm by his actions, and he wanted her to know that.

But more than an apology, Khamil wanted to be there for her. If there was anything he could do to help her, he would.

"Monique

Khamil turned and glanced out the other window,

Eight

Days after the airing of her mother's story on *America's Most Wanted,* several tips had come in, but none were promising. Still, police investigators in New York and Toronto were looking into the various leads.

"It's going to take time," the detective from the Ontario Provincial Police had told Monique earlier today.

She understood that, but still, she was impatient. The longer it took, the less chance there was of the crime being solved. And she'd already been waiting for sixteen years.

"Afternoon, Harry," Monique said to the doorman as she entered her building, but she wasn't her cheerful self. Maybe she'd put too much hope in this television show being able to reach someone who'd miraculously know something about her mother's death.

"Good afternoon, Ms. Savard," Harry responded, smiling brightly as usual. "Away in some exotic locale again?"

"I guess so, if you call Los Angeles exotic." She'd left bright and early Sunday morning, right after the airing of *America's Most Wanted* the previous Saturday night.

"Palm trees . . ." Harry smiled, making his middle-aged face light up with the excitement of a young boy's. "I'd call that exotic."

"Don't forget the smog," Monique joked.

"That's why I'm moving to Florida when I retire. Plus, it's a lot less expensive."

"True," Monique agreed.

As she stepped past Harry, he turned and said, "There's a package for you in the office."

"Thank you, Harry."

"My pleasure. Glad to have you back."

Couriered packages often arrived for her, and because she was busy, they were left in the office when she wasn't at home to personally receive them. Stepping into the lobby, Monique first went to her mailbox, where she retrieved a handful of mail. There were a couple of flyers, which she discarded in the nearby trash can. And a couple of bills.

Next, she went to the apartment's office, where she picked up the package that had been sent for her. One look at it and she knew it was from her agency. No doubt, this package held the new contract for the runway show she would do in France next month.

Walking back to the lobby, Monique slipped a finger beneath the envelope's tab, opening the flap as she headed to the elevator. Absently, she pressed the elevator's up button.

She glanced inside the envelope. Yep, it looked like a contract. But there was something else that caught her eye.

Inside the package was also a mauve envelope. Puzzled, Monique reached for it and pulled it out. It immediately struck her as odd, because it looked as though it held a card, and her agent wasn't prone to sending cards with contracts.

It *was* a card, she realized, just as the elevator door

opened. A young couple stepped off, and Monique entered, then hit the button for the penthouse floor.

A Post-It note was stuck to the envelope, on which Elaine Cox had written *This came for you. No return address.*

It wasn't unusual for Monique to receive fan mail from her agency, but usually there were several pieces instead of one.

As the elevator ascended, Monique opened the envelope and withdrew the card. It had a floral picture on the front and the words *I'm thinking of you.*

Monique opened the card.

Instantly, her heart went into overdrive. Panic seized every nerve in her body.

Inside was written *Just the way I thought of your mother.*

Frantically, Monique searched the envelope again, knowing it would yield no clue as to where it had come from. But what did it mean? Clearly, someone was trying to taunt her—but why? And who?

The person who had stalked her mother?

Monique didn't realize the elevator door had opened until it started to close. Quickly, she jumped out and onto her floor. Then she looked both right and left down the hallway, a chill sweeping over her.

Her mother had received numerous cards and letters from some deranged psycho before her death, those letters also going to her agent.

But there was nothing overtly sinister about this card, nor its contents. Still, she couldn't help feeling creepy.

Monique hurried down the hallway to her door, then opened it as fast as she could and rushed inside. Was Daniel right—was she asking for more trouble in her life than she could handle, all because she was obsessed with finding her mother's killer?

Or was this letter from someone who had seen *America's Most Wanted,* and simply wanted to let her know she was in this person's thoughts? Not everyone was articulate and expressed exactly what they meant.

Still, as Monique locked and bolted her door, she almost heard the bubble bursting around the illusion of her safety.

Her mother hadn't been safe from the person who had wanted to hurt her. Why had she ever believed she would be?

The sound of the ringing telephone instantly woke Monique, making her wonder when she'd drifted off to sleep. Straightening herself on her plush sofa, she reached for the phone on the adjacent end table. "Hello?"

"Monique."

"Dad!" Monique exclaimed, elated to finally hear her father s voice. "Where have you been? I've left several messages for you."

"I could ask you the same thing."

"I've been out of town for a few days," Monique replied. She'd tried calling her father while away on business, but realized she hadn't called home to check her messages. "I was in Los Angeles shooting a commercial. I tried calling you while I was away."

"You know I don't like answering my phone unless I know who's calling. If the ID box doesn't say, I don't pick up."

"Yeah, I know." Not answering the phone was a habit her father had begun in the months after his wife's death, as all the calls were either from reporters or police telling him not to leave town. Now, even though that had all happened years ago, he hadn't gotten out of the habit. Which saddened Monique. He'd closed himself off from most of the world, as surely as if a big piece of him had died the night his wife had.

"So," Monique said, "how are you?"

"I'm still hanging in," he replied. "But what I'm really curious about is that message you left me. The police are reopening your mother's murder case?"

"Yes." Unable to reach her father before now, Monique had left him minimal details. Now, she filled him in on everything.

"I saw the show," he told her.

"You did?" Monique asked. "I thought maybe you were away, since you didn't answer your phone, and you didn't get back to me that night."

"No, I got your message all right."

"But you were upset with me," Monique said.

"A little, I guess."

"Dad, I know I should have told you about all this before any of it happened, but . . . Well, I was afraid of what you'd say. I know how much you want to put all this behind you, but the truth is, I can't. I have to do everything I can to see Mom's killer brought to justice."

Her father let out a long, sad sigh. "Oh, sweetie. You're so young, so full of hope. I wish I could believe that after all this time there could finally be an answer, but I don't trust the police. You know that, and you know why."

She did know why; her father had gone through hell as the prime suspect. Even now, his name hadn't officially been cleared. Still, there were many ways a crime could be solved, including witnesses coming forward after several years. She told her father that.

"We'll see, sweetie."

"Dad, this isn't only for Mom. This is for you, too. To clear your name."

"Which is why I can't be mad with you about not telling me sooner. I know you always have the best intentions. But I'm just so tired of it all."

And he'd stopped living because of it. He'd stopped fighting for justice, because clearing his own name had required so much of him, and still he hadn't been able to successfully do that.

"Well, the police may want to question you again, depending on how the investigation goes."

"I told them all I had to tell them for two years," her father said defensively. "I ain't gonna tell them no more."

"Dad . . ."

"I'm serious, Monique. Look, you do what you have to do, and I'm gonna do what I have to do. I've had enough stress to last ten lifetimes."

"I know it hasn't been easy—"

"There's nothing I can tell the police that they don't already know. And I don't want them to consider me a suspect again, whenever they get good and ready." He paused. "You didn't tell them where I am, did you?"

"No, but—"

"Good. Then please, promise me you won't."

Monique hesitated. "Dad, they never charged you with Mom's murder before. I doubt they will now."

"They think because we used to argue a lot, that means I killed her," Lucas Savard said, almost as if he was speaking to himself. "No, I won't allow myself to be the victim of another witch-hunt."

"Dad, what if they *need* to talk to you?"

"Promise me, Monique. Promise me you won't tell them how to reach me."

For a moment, Monique remembered what Doreen had said, that she was naive to not even consider the possibility that her father had killed her mother. Was she naive? Did her father have something to hide?

"You know the police can find you if they need to."

"If that's the case, then so be it. But you don't tell them where I am. You hear?"

Monique didn't answer.

"Promise me, Monique. I can't go through this again, all for another disappointment."

Monique exhaled a weary breath. "All right, Dad. I promise you."

As Monique hung up, she had an uneasy feeling in her gut. Did her father simply want to be left alone because he'd endured so much, or did he in fact have something to hide?

The question of her father's guilt or innocence bothered Monique long after she hung up the phone. Until now, she'd always been convinced of her father's innocence. Not that she wasn't anymore . . . she just wasn't sure.

The thought of her father, a man she loved and admired, killing her mother was too much to bear. And she had to ask herself if her resistance to even considering him a suspect was due to an inability to believe that someone she loved so much could do something so horrible.

Monique paced the floor in her penthouse suite, moving to peer through the blinds. Below, she saw people strolling, walking their dogs, and jogging through Central Park. She'd always felt safe here, but it seemed everything she once believed about her life was shattering like glass around her.

Groaning, she pivoted on her heel, marching back

into the living room. She wouldn't do this anymore. If her father had killed her mother, she would *know* it. She'd have to.

Her mind drifted to the card she'd received, and her shoulders drooped with relief. Of course her father hadn't killed her mother. Her theory had always been that her mother's stalker had committed the crime.

Her moment of relief dissipated as the reality of her thoughts hit her full force. If it was a stalker, then that stalker could still be out there. He could be the one who'd sent her the card. And if he'd sent her the card . . .

Monique dropped herself onto the sofa, then buried her face in her hands. She'd been planning to head out tonight, to meet her friends at Angel's, but what if someone truly wanted to hurt her? What if someone knew her routine?

What she needed was a distraction, something else to think about, before paranoia got the better of her. Picking up the telephone's receiver, she decided to check for messages.

"Monique." Her heart instantly fluttered at the sound of Khamil's deep, sexy voice. "This is Khamil. I just saw *America's Most Wanted*, and figured I'd give you a call. I . . . I had no clue. Call me when you can."

There were a total of three messages from Khamil, all in which he called to see how she was doing and asked her to call him. The fact that he cared enough to call after seeing the show touched her heart. Perhaps because her own family members didn't seem to support or understand her quest for justice, it was refreshing to hear from someone who cared enough for her to talk about it.

Monique found Khamil's number, then lifted the

receiver and dialed the phone. She was about to hang up when she heard Khamil answer the phone.

"Hello?"

Monique swallowed, then said, "Hi."

"Monique?"

"Yeah," she answered softly.

"I saw the show," Khamil said before she had a chance to say anything else. "I'm sorry."

"Thanks," Monique replied.

Khamil wanted to ask why she hadn't told him, though he knew why. They were barely getting to know each other. So he said, "If there's anything I can do to help, let me know."

"I appreciate that."

"You want to talk about it?"

Monique blew out a weary sigh. "There's not much more to tell other than what you saw. My mother was murdered sixteen years ago and the killer has never been apprehended."

"But the police are reopening the case?"

"Yes. I'm not sure why, but I can only pray that this time, the killer is caught."

There was a pause; then Khamil said, "I must say, I'm surprised that you became a model, like your mother. If indeed it was a stalker who killed her . . ."

"I know," Monique said softly. "None of my family understands that. I'm not even sure I understand it myself. But I don't want my mother's legacy to die, and if there's a chance I can catch her killer—"

"Wait a second," Khamil interjected. "What do you mean by that?" When Monique didn't answer, he continued. "Are you trying to say that you're *hoping* your mother's killer will come after you?"

Khamil felt a jolt of fear in his gut when Monique didn't answer. "Monique, that's crazy."

"I don't know what I'm trying to do," Monique

finally said. "All I know is that I want my mother's killer caught."

"I can understand that. But not at the risk of putting yourself in danger."

"Khamil—"

"Monique," Khamil responded firmly. Then he paused. It wasn't up to him to tell her what to do, but he certainly didn't want to see her put herself at risk.

After a long moment, Khamil said, "Let the police do their job."

Monique didn't respond at first, and Khamil wondered if he'd offended her. But then she said, "I appreciate you caring. Honestly. Sometimes it seems like I'm the only one in my family who wants justice."

"I have to apologize for something."

"What?" Monique sounded surprised.

"You made a comment about me seeming like a stalker to you that night when I saw you at Angel's. Now I see . . . I realize that I probably really scared you. Given what happened to your mother."

"Oh. Well . . ." Truthfully, she hadn't thought of Khamil as a stalker. If she had, she never would have kissed him. The sudden thought of the kiss they'd shared made her feel hot. Lord help her, here they were discussing her mother's murder, and she was suddenly feeling hot remembering a kiss that didn't mean anything. What was wrong with her?

"It's no big deal," Monique finished. "I'm sure I overreacted."

"Still, I shouldn't have come on so strong, so please, know that it won't happen again."

Khamil's words should have reassured her, but instead Monique's stomach lurched, a queasy feeling washing over her as she held the phone. Why was she disappointed? She'd flat out told Khamil that she didn't appreciate his advances, yet part of her didn't want to hear that he'd never come on to her again. Surely there was something wrong with her.

"Uh-huh."

"All right," Khamil said. He wanted to invite Monique to a café where they could talk some more, but that was hardly appropriate right now. Besides, she'd made it clear she wasn't interested, so why couldn't he simply let go?

He'd always been too analytical, searching for a reason for everything. And right now, his brain told him that maybe, just maybe, Monique would give him a chance to really get to know her if it weren't for her mother's unsolved murder. She was stunning, and he sensed a fiery passion within her, but he also sensed that she was a no-nonsense type of woman who wouldn't spend her days and nights indulging in romance when something as serious as her mother's murder hung over her head.

"I've got some work to do, so I'm gonna let you go," Khamil said. "But please, if you ever need to talk about anything, do give me a call."

"Sure," Monique agreed.

Then Khamil hung up, and Monique felt a measure of sadness. Why was she suddenly feeling drawn to him?

No doubt because he was offering to be there for her, and she often felt as though she had no one.

Maybe she had judged him too harshly, thinking him only a playboy out to add more notches to his bedpost.

Well, she knew one thing for sure. She did appreciate his offer, and if and when she needed to talk, she wouldn't hesitate to call him.

Nine

"Hey, if there's somewhere else you've gotta be, just tell me."

Whipping his head around, Khamil stared at his brother, Javar, who sat across the table from him at Angel's. "What? Why would you say that?"

Javar shrugged. "You keep looking at your watch, like there's somewhere else you've got to be."

"Naw," Khamil said, reaching for his mug of beer. "I don't have anything else to do."

"Then you must not miss your big brother."

"Older, not bigger." Khamil flashed a wry grin, then flexed an arm, displaying a huge muscle even beneath his long-sleeved white shirt. He'd played football in high school and college, while Javar's sport of choice had been basketball. As a result, Javar had a slimmer build than Khamil. "And why would you say I don't miss you?"

"Because if you have nowhere else to go, then you must be pretty bored with my company."

"What?" Khamil's eyebrows shot together, confused.

"You seem more interested in everyone else in this place."

"Huh?" But as Khamil asked the question, he instinctively glanced over his shoulder, then back at his brother.

"That's what I'm talking about," Javar said. "You looking all over the place like you're bored with the company."

Khamil straightened himself in the seat, resting his elbows on the table. "No, man. Of course not. I'm not bored. Just checking out the place."

Javar settled back in his chair and stared at Khamil. "Ah. I get it. You're expecting someone."

"Now you're tripping." Khamil's lips curled in a slight smile. "How could I be expecting someone when I'm here with you?"

"Okay, then." Javar took a swig of his beer. "You were saying?"

Javar placed the mug back on the table. "Probably nothing that would interest you. At least not yet, little brother. Since you still refuse to settle down."

Khamil flashed his brother a mock-scowl. "Try me."

"Remember Derrick, Whitney's old school friend?"

"The cop who kept sweating you because he thought you were the one threatening Whitney's life?"

"Yeah."

"He's not still in love with Whitney, is he?"

"Naw," Javar replied. "He and Whitney are just friends."

"You sure about that?"

"Yep," Javar replied confidently. "He got married a couple years ago to a woman he was investigating for murder. But that's a whole other story."

"Wow."

"She wasn't guilty, of course. Anyway, Derrick fell in love with her—Samona's her name—they got married, and now he and Samona are expecting. In fact, she's due about two weeks before Whitney."

"Really?"

"Mmm-hmm. Samona and Whitney have become really close. In fact, I never thought it was possible, but Derrick and I have become good friends, too. Anyway, it's been quite an experience with the two of them being pregnant together—you can imagine the kinds of plans they're making for the new babies. They're driving me and Derrick crazy!"

A smile touched Khamil's lips as he watched his brother's eyes light up. Man, had it really been years since they'd both been single, hanging out in Chicago's hottest nightclubs? Back then, they'd talked about all the honeys, Khamil jokingly lamenting over the fact that there weren't enough hours in a day for him to date all the women he wanted. Now, here Javar was talking about pregnancies and family stuff.

"Sounds like you're loving every minute of it, J."

Javar's lips spread in a wide grin. "Yeah, I am. Now, I'm just waiting for you to make me an uncle."

"Michelle's already made you an uncle."

"I'm not talking about our sister. I'm talking about you." Javar lifted his beer glass, tipping it slightly in Khamil's direction as if to punctuate his point. "You can't be a playboy forever."

"Just because I'm single at thirty-eight doesn't make me a playboy."

"Ha." Javar chuckled. "I know you."

The sound of female laughter caught Khamil's attention, and once again he turned toward the door. Instantly, he felt a nervous tickle in his stomach as he saw Vicky and a couple of the other models enter the restaurant. After a beat, he realized Monique wasn't with them. She always hung out with this group at Angel's on Thursday nights, so where was she?

If not for learning that someone had murdered her mother, Khamil might not be concerned. But he found he was worried about Monique. He hoped she was okay.

Khamil was pushing his chair back when Javar said, "Hey, where are you going?"

"Excuse me a minute," Khamil said absently. He stood, then headed toward the models' table, determined to find out where Monique was.

Monique jumped out of the cab and ran toward the front door of Angel's, taking a quick glance around at the crowded Times Square sidewalk before entering the restaurant. Her heart raced frantically, and she was in no mood for a casual get-together, but she had no clue where else to go.

All she knew was that right now, she was too afraid to be alone.

"Hello, Monique," Aaron, the host said. "The gang's already here at your usual table."

Monique managed a faint smile and nod before rushing past the host. But suddenly, she stopped midstride as she rounded the corner and saw Vicky and Khamil in an embrace.

Her stomach churned at the sight, and for a moment, she was so stunned, she didn't move.

Khamil and Vicky pulled apart. As if he sensed her presence, Khamil spun around, his eyes meeting hers.

Monique stared at him for only a brief second before turning and heading back toward the front door.

"Monique," Khamil called.

Monique didn't stop, instead picking up her pace.
But a waitress carrying a tray of food was in her
path, and she was forced to slow down as she tried
to dodge past the woman.

"Monique, hold up."

Monique ignored Khamil as she stepped to the
side, allowing the waitress to pass. However, before
she could continue walking, she felt a hand on her
shoulder.

Though she knew it was Khamil, she turned anyway. Frowning at him, she shrugged away from his
touch, then started off.

"Monique, wait." Khamil's fingers curled around
her wrist.

Monique blew out a frustrated breath, then faced
Khamil. "What?"

He looked down at her with concern. "You tell me."

"Nothing."

Khamil linked fingers with hers, as if he'd held
her hand like this a million times. And damn if she
didn't feel a flush of warmth through her body at
his touch. Still, she glared at him. "What do you
think you're doing?"

Khamil moved in front of her, leading her toward
the front door. "We're going to talk."

Monique wanted to yank her hand from Khamil's,
but several of the restaurant patrons around them
were staring at them, and she didn't want to make
a spectacle of herself. So she allowed Khamil to lead
her outside. Several people of all ages swarmed the
sidewalks in Times Square, some casually strolling,
while others walked briskly. Khamil dodged the mass
of people and led Monique to the sidewalk's edge.
Once there, she pulled her hand free.

"Monique, what's wrong?"

"Nothing," she lied.

"No, something's obviously bothering you. Are you okay?"

As she stared up at him, a lump formed in her throat. No, she wasn't okay. The last time she'd spoken to Khamil, she'd decided that she'd judged him too harshly, that perhaps he wasn't a shallow playboy. But seeing him all over Vicky . . .

This was stupid. Here she was, getting upset about a man she wasn't even dating, when her main concern should be the letter she'd received today. Another letter had arrived today, making the fear that someone was stalking her a reality. The letter might not have bothered her so much if it hadn't arrived at her apartment.

Khamil placed both hands on Monique's shoulders. "Monique?" Her eyes were slightly bulged, and Khamil's stomach knotted with concern. Something had happened. "God, tell me . . ."

"I got a letter," she answered after a few moments.

"A letter? What kind of letter?"

Monique reached into her small purse and withdrew an envelope. Wondering what was going on, Khamil took the envelope from her hands. He lifted the flap and withdrew a folded sheet of paper.

> *Every day, I think about you.*
> *Every night, I dream about you.*
> *You don't know it, but I watch you.*
> *I see you everywhere, and you enthrall me,*
> *just like your mother did . . .*

The moment Khamil finished reading the letter, he asked, "Where did you get this?"

Monique wrapped her arms around her torso, as if cold, even though the late spring evening was warm. "It came in the mail."

"To your *place?*" As Khamil asked the question, he checked out the envelope. It was addressed to Monique, and had been mailed via the U.S. Postal Service.

"Yeah."

"This is bad." Khamil pressed a palm against his bald head as he contemplated the seriousness of the situation.

"It's the second one."

"Second?"

Monique nodded brusquely.

"Have you gone to the police yet?"

"No. I just . . . I came straight here when I got that."

"Monique, you have to go to the police. Especially if this is the second letter."

"The first one went to my agent, so I didn't worry much about it. Besides, it wasn't threatening, at least not overtly."

"But this one went to your place."

"Yes."

"So this person obviously knows where you live."

Monique's bottom lip trembled, and she bit down on it. Then she said, "Okay, I'll go to the police. Then I'll let the doorman at my building know about this."

"You're not going back there."

Monique's eyes flew to Khamil's. "What?"

There was no way Khamil was going to let Monique go back home if there was even a hint of danger to her. "You'll come to my place."

While just a moment ago Monique's lip had trembled with fear, defiance now flashed in her eyes. "Really? You *tell* me I'm going back to your place, and that's just it."

"I'm not going to let you go home."

"Khamil, you can't tell me what to do."

"This is serious, Monique. And I don't want to see you hurt."

An image of Khamil and Vicky in an embrace flashed in Monique's mind. "Fine. I appreciate that. But I can go somewhere else besides your place."

Khamil shook his head, dismissing that thought.

"Why are you shaking your head?" Monique asked. "You have no right to tell me what to do."

"Look, Monique, I'd just feel a lot better if you stayed with me. We can go back to your place and pick up some stuff you'll need, then head to my place."

Monique planted both hands on her hips. "In case you haven't realized, this is the year 2001—not the Stone Age."

Khamil held up both hands, as if in surrender. "Look, I know you have a right to make your own decisions. I'm not trying to tell you what to do. But . . ." Khamil's voice trailed off, as he brought a hand to Monique's face and gently stroked it. "Do you have a better idea?"

Monique's face tingled where Khamil's fingers had just been. "I . . . I could go to one of my girlfriends' places."

"Monique, if someone is after you, watching you as they say, then another woman won't be a deterrent. I'm not trying to be sexist, but I'm a big guy. I don't think anyone would mess with you if I was around."

At his words, Monique's gaze fell to his muscular chest and arms. Yes, Khamil was a big guy. In fact, he could easily be mistaken for a football player. He was right. No one would bother her if he was with her.

Still, she said, "I don't want to be an inconvenience."

"Monique, I won't be able to sleep for worrying about you."

"I see." Monique wanted to ask why he cared so much, but she didn't. Some men liked to be heroes, to protect those who needed protection. She didn't want to read more into his concern than that. "Will you have to explain my being there to anyone?"

"Like a girlfriend?"

Glancing away, Monique nodded.

"If that's your way of asking if I'm involved with anyone, the answer is no. But you should know that by now."

Of course he didn't have a serious girlfriend. He was too busy playing with several.

"So," Khamil began after a moment, "you'll come to my place?"

"Sure."

Khamil's mouth curled in a smile. "Great. I've got to go back inside and tell my brother I'm leaving."

"Your brother?"

"Yeah. We were about to have dinner."

"Khamil, I don't want to keep you from your dinner."

"It's okay."

"Why don't we do this—you have dinner with your brother, I'll eat something with my friends, and then we can hook up to head to your place."

Khamil paused, considering her suggestion. After a moment, he said, "Sure. That makes sense. Besides, my brother's only in town for a couple days."

"Khamil, like I told you, I can go to someone else's place."

"Don't worry about it. My brother's got work to do anyway, so it's not a big deal."

"All right. If you're sure."

"I am."

Monique gave Khamil a tentative smile, and warmth spread in Khamil's stomach. Funny that a smile could touch him in such a way, but perhaps hers made him feel good because she hadn't really given him one before.

Khamil placed a hand on the small of her back, and was about to guide her toward the door when he noticed a black car speeding toward them. Something made his heart race at the sight, instantly fearing the worst, while hoping it wouldn't be.

But when the car mounted the curb and headed straight toward them, every nerve in Khamil's body screamed.

Then so did Monique.

Ten

A scream tore from Monique's throat when she realized the out-of-control black car was headed straight for them.

"Get down!" Khamil yelled a mere instant before he tackled her to the ground. Tires squealed as the car burned rubber off the sidewalk and back onto the road, speeding away.

It took Monique a full few seconds to realize what had happened; then she cried, "Oh, my God! Oh, my God!" Glancing at the road, she saw the tail end of the late-model sedan just before it darted in front of another car and disappeared.

"Are you okay?" There was a note of anxiety in Khamil's voice.

Her breathing ragged, Monique looked up into Khamil's dark eyes, eyes that were filled with both fear and concern. She managed a small nod, then, "Ow."

"What?" Khamil asked.

"My arm."

"Sorry," Khamil said, realizing that his full weight was on her slender body. Easing up, he saw that Monique was positioned partly on her side and partly on her back, one arm pressed against the sidewalk.

A crowd started to form around Khamil and Monique as Khamil rose to his feet. Monique sat up slowly, as though with difficulty. He watched her chest heave as she inhaled and exhaled, watched the dazed expression on her face, and something in his gut ached. What if he hadn't been able to get her out of the way in time?

Khamil reached for her and pulled her to her feet. She collapsed against his chest, and he wrapped a comforting arm around her.

"You two all right?" a man in the crowd asked.

Khamil glanced down at Monique. She nodded. "I'm . . . fine."

"I can't believe this," Khamil muttered. Then, to the people surrounding them, he asked, "Did anyone get a look at the plate?"

People shook their heads.

"Damn," Khamil said. He pulled Monique closer, as though he'd held her like this a thousand times. She felt good in his arms, and he felt good knowing that she trusted him to give her support. He didn't know why, but her trust in him mattered more than it had ever mattered where a woman was concerned before.

"Khamil, what happened?" Monique asked. Her voice was shaky, and as he held her, he realized that her body was slightly trembling.

What *had* happened? Khamil suddenly wondered. Had the driver been on a cell phone and not paying attention? Or had he deliberately tried to run them over? The letter Monique had received had Khamil wondering if the near accident was actually an accident after all.

Before Khamil could answer her question, he saw Javar hustling toward him. "What the hell happened?" his brother asked.

"Some jerk mounted the curb and nearly hit us,"

Khamil replied. Thinking of just how close the car had come to hitting them, Khamil gritted his teeth.

"New York drivers," Javar lamented, then shook his head.

Monique's gaze went from Khamil to this other man. Though he had a slimmer build, he had a narrow face, like Khamil's, as well as deep-set eyes. There was a definite resemblance between the two men. This had to be Khamil's brother.

The man's eyes met hers, and he smiled, then threw a suspicious glance toward Khamil. "So, Khamil," he began in a sing-song voice, "who's this?"

"Oh. Javar, this is a friend, Monique. Monique, this is my brother, Javar."

"Nice to meet you," Monique said, extending a hand.

Javar shook it. "Nice to meet you as well. So, you're the reason my brother deserted me at our table."

"We were just heading back inside," Khamil commented.

Javar's lips curled in a sly grin. "Mmm-hmm."

Khamil gave his brother a don't-go-there look. He could tell by his brother's lopsided grin that his brain was working overtime, trying to assess the nature of his relationship with Monique.

Javar leaned in close and whispered in Khamil's ear. "She's beautiful, man."

Khamil just nodded. "All right, you ready for some dinner?"

"Actually, I'm cool. I can pick up a burger, or order room service from the hotel."

"Oh, no," Monique interjected. "I don't want to ruin your dinner plans."

Javar waved off her concern. "Don't worry about

me." To Khamil, he added, "Go ahead and hang
out with your lady friend."

The inflection in Javar's tone said he thought she
and Khamil had a relationship. She was about to correct him, but didn't bother. Instead, she said, "Will
you both excuse me?"

Khamil's eyes met hers with concern. "Where are
you going?"

"Inside. I'm gonna tell the girls I won't be hanging out tonight." At the thought of her friends, Monique's stomach felt queasy. What was the nature of
Khamil and Vicky's relationship? She wasn't jealous,
but . . . concerned. She didn't want Khamil to lead
her on, making her think he was interested in her,
if in fact he was simply interested in playing the field.
"Give me a minute."

"Sure," Khamil agreed.

When Monique disappeared inside the restaurant,
Javar slapped him hard on the back. "So, little
brother, something you've been keeping from me?"

Shaking his head, Khamil smirked. "She's a friend,
Javar."

"Uh-oh."

"What?"

"Either you're getting mellow in your old age, or
you've finally been hit by cupid's arrow."

"What?" Khamil made a face.

"When it comes to beautiful women, you never
talk about them in terms of being *friends*. In fact,
you're the first to comment about their various . . .
attributes. And Monique is definitely *fine.*"

"Whatever."

"Mmm-hmm."

"Look, Javar, it's not like that."

Javar merely shrugged. "Well, she seems nice.
Make sure you treat her good."

"Didn't you say you had something to do?" Khamil asked.

Javar chuckled. "Now you want to get rid of me."

"You're a trip, Javar. Give me a call later. We'll try to hook up before you leave town."

Javar wrapped his arms around Khamil in a spontaneous hug. "All right, little brother."

"Younger."

"Whatever."

Maybe she was being paranoid, but the first thing Monique noticed when she joined her friends was the plastic smile Vicky gave her before she took a sip from her water glass.

Monique pulled out the chair beside Renee and slumped onto it.

"What happened?" Renee asked. "You ran out of here like a bat out of hell."

"I . . ." Monique's voice trailed off. How could she admit that she'd run out of the restaurant because she'd seen Vicky and Khamil in an embrace? "I'm a little bit worried."

Janine's eyebrows bunched together. "Why?"

"I've gotten a couple letters recently," Monique told them. "They're not particularly threatening, but they mention my mother. I wouldn't be so worried if the second letter didn't come to my home address."

"Oh, my God," Vicky uttered.

Monique nodded. "I don't know what to make of it, but it gives me the chills." And suddenly the thought hit her that the near accident outside might not have been an accident at all. Good Lord, had someone deliberately tried to run her down?

"Look, sweetie," Renee began. "You've got to go to the police."

"I will." Goose bumps popped out on her skin at the thought that she'd come close to death, and that it may have been a deliberate attempt on her life. Who had tried to run her down, and why?

"Sweetie?" Renee gently rubbed Monique's forearm.

Renee's voice brought Monique back from her thoughts. "I don't feel much like hanging tonight."

"What's Khamil saying?"

At Vicky's question, Monique's eyes flew to hers. Yes, there was something strange about Vicky tonight. Her eyes were bright, yet they didn't hold the warmth they normally did. "Khamil says I should go to the police."

"Hmm." Vicky gave a brief nod, though she didn't seem satisfied with Monique's answer.

"In fact, we're gonna do that now." Monique pushed her chair back and stood.

"Khamil's gonna go with you?" Vicky asked.

"Mmm-hmm."

There was that plastic smile again. "Yeah, Khamil's a real gentleman."

Until now, Monique had never had a problem with Vicky, though she'd heard from some other girls at the agency that Vicky could be a back-stabber. She had a reputation for going after what she wanted and not caring who she hurt. Monique had taken those rumors with a grain of salt. But now she had to wonder if Vicky, a woman she'd had as a friend for the past five years, would actually let something like a man come between them.

Because this *was* about Khamil. Monique knew that, even if Vicky wouldn't admit it.

"Tell Khamil we said good-bye," Vicky said, her

upbeat tone contrary to the negative vibes she was sending Monique's way.

"Sure." Monique forced a grin. "I'll see you all later."

"Bye," Renee and Janine replied in unison.

"See ya." Vicky wriggled her fingers at Monique, then turned to Renee and Janine.

Monique turned and walked away.

"What's the matter?" Khamil asked.

"Nothing," Monique replied, but her tone was clipped. She and Khamil were in the elevator in her building, heading back downstairs. At her apartment, she'd collected some clothes and essential items.

Khamil placed a hand on her shoulder, and Monique jumped. "Monique." Khamil's voice was gentle. "It's going to be okay."

Monique didn't respond, instead staring straight ahead. Her mind was filled with so many doubts. Doubts about her mother's murder, and about who was possibly sending the letters. And as she tried to avoid eye contact with Khamil, she knew she also had doubts about him. Some moments, like right now, he could seem so gentle and compassionate, but then other moments, she didn't know if he was a thoughtless playboy.

It doesn't matter, she told herself. She couldn't allow herself to care about Khamil, anyway. Raymond had told her that she'd been too obsessed with finding her mother's killer to commit to someone, and maybe he was right.

Raymond. Monique's heart fluttered as she thought of him. He hadn't called her in more than a week, hadn't dropped by Angel's. Had he finally gotten the point—or had he resorted to another tactic? He'd already tried to entice her back into a relationship with him by implying that he had information about her mother. How far would he go to get her back in his life?

"Monique."

Drifting back from her thoughts to the present, she looked at Khamil. He was pressing a hand against the open elevator door. Monique stepped past him off the elevator.

Harry gave her a bright smile. "Hello, Monique."

"Hello." Monique sauntered toward him. "Harry, has anyone come her looking for me—anyone you haven't seen before?"

Harry shook his head. "No."

"What about Raymond? Has he come around?"

Again, Harry shook his head. "I haven't seen him." He paused. "Is there a problem?"

"No, no." If Raymond hadn't been around, nor anyone else, there was no point in mentioning anything. At least not yet. "Just curious."

"Well, you let me know if I can be of any help to you."

"Sure," Monique told him.

When she felt a hand on her shoulder, Monique whipped around, slightly startled. She knew Khamil was with her, so why was she so on edge around him?

Maybe because he was too touchy-feely. And she suddenly couldn't help wondering if he was like this with every woman, or if he was being like this with just her.

"You want to get a bite to eat before we head to my place?"

A tingling sensation spread over Monique's skin. Such a simple question, but it conjured up all sorts of illicit thoughts in her mind.

And then she couldn't help wondering how casually Khamil invited other women over, women he ended up making love to . . .

Good Lord, what was wrong with her? There was no decent reason for her to be thinking of Khamil's private life, because it was none of her business. Besides, she wasn't heading to his place for sex.

"Maybe this isn't a good idea."

Monique didn't realize she'd spoken aloud until Khamil asked, "Why not?"

"The truth is, Khamil, I hardly know you." Monique spoke as she opened the lobby doors and stepped outside, partly because she didn't want to face him. There was something about his eyes when he looked at her that unnerved her.

"I think you know enough."

"Enough?" Still, Monique didn't turn, instead starting down the street.

Khamil kept pace with her. "Are we talking, or are we walking? Monique, if you'll slow down . . ."

She quickened her pace, knowing she must seem foolish, but she couldn't stop herself. Spending the night at Khamil's place suddenly seemed very dangerous.

Khamil placed a firm hand on her arm, and Monique stopped, the fight gone out of her. Slowly, Khamil turned her around, drew her body to his.

And then he covered her mouth with his, urgently kissing her. Monique kissed him back with just as much fervor, her hands slipping around his neck, his slipping around her waist. Their tongues mingled, their hands explored, the passion between them as strong and undeniable as if it had caught them in a web.

Panting, Monique finally pulled away. This was exactly what she didn't want.

"Monique . . ." Khamil's voice was husky, filled with desire.

"What was that?" she asked, looking around as if she'd heard something that had startled her.

"What?"

When Khamil glanced around to see what she was talking about, Monique slipped out of his arms. Trying to ignore the reality that she now missed his embrace, she hustled to the edge of the sidewalk. Thankfully, a cab was approaching, and she flung her hand in the air to hail it.

"Yo, Monique." Again, Khamil placed a hand on her arm, but she shrugged away from his touch. As the cab came to a stop, she opened the back door and jumped inside. Without another word, Khamil followed her.

"Where to?" the driver asked as they settled in their seats.

Khamil looked at Monique, but she didn't meet his eyes. So much for getting her input. "There's a little jazz bar on fifty-seventh. A new establishment."

"I know the place," the driver said, his upbeat tone indicating he'd been there.

Facing Khamil, Monique guffawed. "Khamil, I'm not exactly up for dinner and jazz tonight."

There was something about her resistance that challenged him, challenged the side of him that had always been a joker. As a child, he'd irked more than one teacher with his class clown antics, and when he'd started liking girls, he'd shown his interest in them by teasing them.

He raised an eyebrow at Monique and said, "In a hurry to get to my place, darling?"

Muttering something unintelligible, Monique fell back against the seat and stared out the taxi's window.

Khamil turned and glanced out the other window, hiding his smirk. What had gotten into him? He felt as if he were in sixth grade again, teasing Cecelia Mathers. But he also felt a measure of satisfaction, because, like Cecelia, Monique's hot and cold routine around him told exactly what he wanted to know.

She wanted him. Just as much as he wanted her.

Feeling her eyes upon him, Khamil faced Monique. Quick as lightning, her head spun in the other direction. No doubt, she was hoping he hadn't noticed her staring at him. However, she hadn't turned away fast enough.

A soft chuckle fell from Khamil's lips. It was going to be an interesting night.

Eleven

Monique pulled at the neck of her shirt, holding it from her body to allow her skin to breathe. Lord, it was hot in here! It wasn't even summer yet and here she was, sweating.

She stole a glance at Khamil, his smug smirk making her angry. Why was she allowing him to get to her like this? She didn't have time for his games.

She blew out a hot breath. God, there was no fresh air in this car. She hit the window's power button, opening the window to let fresh air in as the taxi drove.

Khamil leaned in close and whispered, "I know. It's getting hot in here."

The low timbre of his voice caused a tremor to pass through Monique's body. She didn't dare say a word to Khamil, didn't dare look his way. There was no way she was going to give him the satisfaction of knowing that he'd gotten under her skin. She could only hope her cool exterior masked the desire burning within her.

Because that's exactly what was happening, she realized with chagrin. The more time she spent with Khamil, the less she could deny that there was something about him that made her blood stir. At first, she'd told herself that he made her blood stir in a bad way, because he irritated her. So what if she'd felt a tingle in places she hadn't in ages after their first kiss? She'd simply ignored that. But after the last kiss, she could no longer deny that Khamil made every cell in her body come alive in a way she hadn't ever experienced before.

Even if she didn't like it.

Not that she didn't like the feeling; she just didn't like the man.

When the taxi pulled up in front of the jazz bar, Monique flinched when she felt Khamil's breath hot on her ear. He asked, "Have you been here before?"

"I don't have much time for socializing."

Khamil raised a suggestive eyebrow. "So I'm the first to take you here."

His darkened gaze made Monique think of other firsts, and once again, she found herself getting hot. But she hoped she maintained her cool front when she asked, "Are you going to pay the driver?"

Khamil held her gaze, slowly drawing his full bottom lip between his teeth. Monique was unable to stop herself from staring, unable to stop her own lips from parting, almost as if she wanted to kiss him again.

She *did* want to kiss him again.

Monique quickly grabbed the door's handle and jumped out of the car.

Khamil watched Monique scramble from the car. Something had changed between them, no doubt about it, and if they didn't have an audience, Khamil would have taken her in his arms and ravished those soft lips of hers until she begged him to make love to her.

He knew just what he would do to her. Starting at her neck, he'd nibble a path to her navel, then lower . . .

"Sir?"

"Huh?" The cab driver's voice was like a splash of cold water—which was exactly what Khamil needed. Damn. Here he was getting hot and hard in the back of a taxi.

"Seven fifty-five."

Khamil dug the wallet out of the back pocket of his pants and handed some bills to the driver. "Keep the change," Khamil told the man.

Monique was already at the restaurant's doors when Khamil got out of the taxi. Her arms crossed over her chest, a frown marred her beautiful features. He felt a stab of disappointment in his gut. What was she afraid of? Was getting to know him such a horrible idea?

Yet he saw a vulnerability in her eyes as he strolled toward her, despite her cold expression.

She's afraid of caring, a voice in his head told him. And he knew it was true. Hadn't he acted the same way after his relationship with Jessica had ended his senior year in college? His family and friends acted as though he'd been incapable of giving his heart, but that wasn't the case. He'd given his heart to Jessica, and she'd broken it. A star college football player at Michigan State with a promising career ahead of him, Khamil's dreams of playing pro ball had ended when a severe hit had dislocated his shoulder. The shoulder hadn't been the same since. Neither had his relationship with Jessica, whom he'd subsequently found in bed with one of his best friends, the quarterback of the team. After finally giving someone his heart and getting burned, Khamil had vowed to never let a woman hurt him again.

And thus far, he'd kept that vow. He'd never given his heart to another woman the way he had to Jessica, and his life had been better for it. Not that he didn't miss the feeling of being in love on occasion, but for the most part, relationships without all the serious emotions had been much less complicated.

So he understood Monique's fear, if she was indeed afraid of getting involved. He had no idea what her past relationships had been like, but he understood that the fact that her mother had been murdered when she was still a child was enough to make her fear getting close to anyone.

"Busy night," Khamil said as he reached Monique, glancing around at the populated street.

"Yeah."

"You ready to go inside?"

In response, Monique turned to the door. She felt so . . . on edge. What was wrong with her? She was an adult; she could handle a dinner with Khamil, couldn't she?

But could she handle spending the night at his place?

Monique's thoughts were interrupted by the sound of laughter. Two women were exiting the restaurant. Both smiled, though their gazes went beyond her, and Monique knew they had to be looking at Khamil. Something inside her stomach tightened painfully, and she couldn't help turning to see how Khamil would react to them.

Khamil returned the women's smiles with a charming one of his own. Monique rolled her eyes, suddenly more irritated than she had the right to be.

"Are you coming?" she quipped.

Khamil's eyes met hers. "What's with the attitude?"

"I'm not the one with the attitude," Monique retorted.

Khamil's gaze narrowed. "If you've got something to say to me, why don't you just say it?"

Monique looked over her shoulder, and satisfied

that no one was within earshot, spoke. "Fine, you're an attractive guy. You obviously know that. But you're taking *me* out to dinner. Is it really that hard for you to put aside your flirtatious ways for such a short time—"

"Flirtatious ways?"

"Do not even try to deny that you were flirting with those women."

Khamil pinned her with his dark eyes. "And that bothers you, does it?"

For a moment, Monique couldn't say anything, almost as if Khamil's eyes had the power to leave her speechless. Trying desperately to concentrate on something other than Khamil's heated gaze, Monique twirled a loose tendril of her ebony hair. She shouldn't have said anything. All she'd done was flatter Khamil's incredibly large ego.

His eyes looked like sparkling black jewels in the dim illumination of the streetlights. "Well?" he prompted.

Monique swallowed. "All I'm trying to say is that it's disrespectful for you to ogle other women when you've got a woman by your side. If you can't understand that—"

"But you're not my woman." Khamil paused. "Or is that the problem—that you want to be?"

Monique was quickly losing control of this situation, but laughed sarcastically to give Khamil the impression that he couldn't be more wrong. "You always have to twist everything to flatter yourself, don't you?"

"Why don't you answer the question?"

"Because that's not the issue—"

"I think it is." Gently, Khamil ran a finger along Monique's jawbone. "I think you want me to look at only you. Only notice your beauty." His finger trailed a path to the soft spot on her neck. "Is that it, Monique? Are you jealous?"

Lord help her, Monique knew she should step away from his touch, but she was unable to move. Why did he have this power over her?

"You couldn't be more wrong," she finally managed to say.

"I'm not so sure about that," Khamil said, but his tone said he was totally sure that she wanted him. "Or are you so used to men looking at you that you don't expect them to look at anyone else?"

Khamil's comment broke the spell he had had her under. Anger swept over Monique, and she stepped away from him, meeting his eyes with cold ones. "I didn't get into this business for the attention, if that's what you're trying to imply."

"But I'm sure you've become accustomed to it. No doubt men all over the world admire your beauty."

Maybe that was part of her problem, she silently conceded. Working in this business, she'd seen how so many men went crazy for a beautiful woman. Yes, she'd rather be beautiful, but she wanted to be appreciated for more than that.

And if an obsessed stalker had killed her mother, then Julia had died because someone had idolized her beauty above all else.

Monique enjoyed modeling, mostly because she was helping to keep her mother's legacy alive. And of course, the money was great. But she had other plans for her life. She couldn't model forever, nor did she want to. Her dream after this career ended was to become an interior designer.

Monique placed her hands firmly on her hips. "I'm not as shallow as you obviously think. And believe me, I know that beauty is more than skin deep."

An important message from the ARABESQUE Editor

Dear Arabesque Reader,

Because you've chosen to read one of our Arabesque romance novels, we'd like to say "thank you"! And, as a special way to thank you, we've selected four more of the books you love so well to send you for FREE!

Please enjoy them with our compliments, and thank you for continuing to enjoy Arabesque...the soul of romance.

Karen Thomas
Senior Editor,
Arabesque Romance Novels

Check out our website at
www.arabesquebooks.com

SPECIAL OFFER!
4 FREE BOOKS

ARABESQUE ®
A PRODUCT OF
★BET BOOKS™

3 QUICK STEPS
TO RECEIVE YOUR "THANK YOU" GIFT
FROM THE EDITOR

Send this card back and you'll receive 4 FREE Arabesque
novels! The introductory shipment of 4 Arabesque novels – a
$23.96 value – is yours absolutely FREE!

There's no catch. You're under no obligation to buy anything.
You'll receive your introductory shipment of 4 Arabesque
novels absolutely FREE (plus $1.50 to offset the costs of
shipping & handling). And you don't have to make any
minimum number of purchases—not even one!

We hope that after receiving your books you'll want to
remain an Arabesque subscriber. But the choice is yours to
continue or cancel, anytime at all! So why not take us up on
our invitation to receive 4 Arabesque Romance Novels, with
no risk of any kind. You'll be glad you did!

Call us
TOLL-FREE
at 1-888-345-BOOK

THE EDITOR'S "THANK YOU" GIFT INCLUDES:

- 4 books absolutely FREE (plus $1.50 for shipping and handling)
- A FREE newsletter, *Arabesque Romance News*, filled with author interviews, book previews, special offers, and more!
- No risks or obligations. You're free to cancel whenever you wish... with no questions asked.

Accepting the four introductory books for FREE (plus $1.50 to offset the cost of shipping & handling) places you under no obligation to buy anything. You may keep the books and return the shipping statement marked "cancelled". If you do not cancel, about a month later we will send 4 additional Arabesque novels, and you will be billed the preferred subscriber's price of just $4.00 per title. That's $16.00 for all 4 books for a savings of 33% off the cover price (Plus $1.50 for shipping and handling). You may cancel at any time, but if you choose to continue, every month we'll send 4 more books, which you may either purchase at the preferred discount price. . . or return to us and cancel your subscription.

THE ARABESQUE ROMANCE CLUB: HERE'S HOW IT WORKS

ARABESQUE ROMANCE BOOK CLUB
P.O. Box 5214
Clifton NJ 07015-5214

PLACE
STAMP
HERE

Monique spoke the last words sharply, her comment no doubt meant for him. Khamil opened his mouth to reply, but the sound of footsteps stopped him. A group of people walked by him and Monique, obviously staring at them, clearly curious as to what was going on. Glancing inside the restaurant, Khamil noticed that the two hostesses in the front were watching them as well.

"What?" Monique asked. She followed Khamil's gaze, but didn't see what had caught his interest.

Facing her, he felt a smile tugging at the corners of his mouth. "Monique, everyone thinks we're having a lovers' quarrel."

Horrified, Monique looked inside the restaurant once more, noting the curious stares of the two hostesses and a couple in the foyer. And when she saw three women approach from across the street, their eyes fixed on them as well, Monique grunted and turned on her heel, ready to walk anywhere but this embarrassing situation.

Khamil's strong fingers wrapped around her slender arm, forcing her to stop. "Honey, will you ever forgive me?" he asked, loud enough for the nosy spectators to hear. A man scurrying by slowed to watch them. Then Khamil pulled Monique into an embrace, squeezing her tightly.

For one fleeting moment, Monique forgot that she was standing in the middle of one of New York's busiest streets, surrounded by curious onlookers. She could only think of how good it felt to be pressed against Khamil's hard body, how right.

But only for a moment.

"Let me go." Monique's voice was soft but her tone was lethal.

"Promise me you'll be nice," Khamil whispered, "and I'll let you go."

Monique closed her eyes, willing the unexpected tantalizing sensation spreading over her body to dissipate. "Just let me go," she said after a moment.

"Not until you promise me that you'll be nice." Khamil's breath was warm against her ear. "Can we both go inside and try to have a nice evening?"

"Forget dinner. Let me go; then you can go home, and I'll go back to my place."

"I'm waiting," was Khamil's reply.

He was really enjoying this! Monique was both furious that she was letting him get to her and embarrassed that people were witnessing this show. This had to end. Now.

"All right," Monique conceded.

"All right what?"

"I'll be nice," Monique quipped. She hoped he was happy. The man was absolutely incorrigible!

Slowly, Khamil released his hold on Monique, but still kept one hand firmly planted around her small waist. With the other hand, he opened the door to the restaurant and led her inside. He smiled at the two hostesses and proudly announced, "It's okay. She forgives me."

"She'd be a fool not to," one hostess muttered to another; then both young women giggled.

Monique forced a smile, though what she really wanted to do was strangle Khamil.

"Table for two?" one of the hostesses asked.

"Yeah," Khamil answered. "Nonsmoking. Something private."

The hostess grabbed two menus. "Right this way."

As Monique and Khamil followed the young woman, Monique whispered, "You are an absolute jerk. And you can let go of me now."

"Not yet."

The hostess led them to a quaint table in the back

corner of the restaurant. "Here you go," she chimed. "I hope this is okay."

"It's fine," Khamil replied.

The hostess placed the two menus on the table, then gave Monique a knowing smile and walked away.

Monique finally jerked her body free of Khamil's strong grasp. She shot an angry look at him, then plopped into her seat.

The smile Monique had once thought charming she now found annoying as Khamil flashed it at her again. "Okay," he said, sitting down. "No more scenes like the one outside."

"I didn't cause that scene," Monique hissed. *"You're* the one—" Monique stopped midsentence and inhaled a frustrated breath. She was going where she didn't want to go. Getting more upset than she already was in the small confines of a restaurant certainly wouldn't do her any good. She needed to relax.

"Maybe I did cause that scene," Khamil admitted. Then he shrugged. "Now we're even." Khamil lifted his menu.

"Even?"

He lowered his menu and pinned her with his eyes. "At Angel's. When you kissed me outside the bathroom. You want to talk about a scene. You gave everyone there something to talk about for weeks."

"Nobody saw us," Monique said softly, suddenly wondering if anyone other than Raymond had seen them. She'd never done anything so . . . shameless.

"Except that guy."

"Right." Monique's tone was sheepish. How could she have been so silly as to kiss Khamil for Raymond's benefit? If she hadn't, she probably wouldn't be here now, dealing with a man she knew she'd be better off staying away from.

"And that's why you kissed me. So he wouldn't bother you."

"We already discussed this."

Khamil rested his elbows on the table and leaned forward. "You know what, Monique? You can deny it all you want, but I know you enjoyed that kiss. You enjoyed me—"

That did it. Monique was *not* going to go there. She shot to her feet faster than Khamil could blink, grabbing her purse and overnight bag as she did. But before she could get away, Khamil grabbed her by the waist and pulled her down onto his lap.

Her breath snagging in her throat, Monique's eyes met Khamil's. Neither said a word, but the moment between them was so intense that it seemed they were the only two people in the world.

"Hey, none of that hanky panky until *after* dinner."

Horrified, Monique looked up to see a pretty Asian woman with long black hair standing over the table with a pen and pad in her hand. "We want to make sure you at least pay the bill," she added, grinning. "Hi, I'm Alice, your server tonight. What can I get you to drink?"

"I'll take a beer," Khamil said. "Whatever you have on tap."

"I'll have a water," Monique told the server. *To throw all over you,* she added silently, glaring at Khamil.

"Bring her a strawberry margarita," Khamil instructed Alice. "She'll like that."

Alice made some notes on her pad, then slipped it in a pocket on her apron. "I'll be right back."

When the waitress was out of earshot, Monique heaved herself off Khamil. "I hope you enjoy the strawberry margarita, because I certainly won't be here to drink it."

"Where are you going to go?" Khamil challenged, his dark eyes daring Monique to answer him. "You know that if you walk out that door, I'll be right on your tail. I'm not letting you go back to your place, Monique. So you may as well stay put, and enjoy your evening."

Knowing he meant every word he said, Monique glared at Khamil for several moments, then slowly sank back into the seat across from him, resigning herself to a night of hell. "Just remember why I'm going to your place tonight."

The waitress returned with their drinks, and Khamil ordered a cheeseburger with fries. Monique decided on an appetizer of chicken fingers.

Monique wasn't big on fruity drinks, preferring a glass of wine to any other type of alcohol. And tonight, she certainly wasn't in the mood to drink at all—certainly not with Khamil. So she fiddled with her straw before finally putting it to her mouth and taking a sip of the strawberry margarita. To her delight, the drink was sweet and refreshing. She took another sip.

"So," Khamil began, "when do you want to go to the police about the letters?"

"I don't know," Monique replied. She'd been considering what she should actually do. "I'm kind of thinking that maybe I'm being premature. I mean, what are the police going to say? The letters aren't truly threatening—"

"The threat is clear, Monique."

"Yes," Monique answered, getting serious. "I guess . . . going to the police will make this all more real."

"You can't ignore this."

"I'm afraid," Monique said softly. Visions of the night she'd found her mother dying on the bedroom floor flashed in her mind. A chill swept over her. Were these two letters possibly from the same person who'd killed her mother?

"I understand that. That's why I'm going to be here for you, Monique. I won't let anything happen to you."

Khamil spoke with confidence, and Monique believed every word he said. She didn't know why, but she did know that he would do whatever he could to keep her safe.

She felt a moment of sadness. Her father hadn't been able to protect her mother. She hadn't been able to save her, either.

"I'll go to the police in the morning," Monique said, fighting the sudden urge to cry.

"Hey." Reaching across the table, Khamil covered one of her hands with his. "It's going to be all right, Monique. I know how important it is for you to get closure, and I'm going to help you do that."

A smile touched Monique's lips. Khamil's words gave her comfort, comfort she desperately needed. Why did he seem to care where her own family did not?

Monique stared into Khamil's eyes, looking for an answer to her question. His dark eyes held compassion. She was confused. One minute she wanted to get away from Khamil, the next she felt like throwing herself in his arms and letting him wash away all her fears. How could he bring out both desires in her?

The waitress arrived with their food then, and both Monique and Khamil ate in silence. When they were finished, Khamil settled the bill; then both he and Monique headed outside, where Khamil hailed a taxi. As a taxi pulled up to the curb, Khamil said, "Last chance. My place, or the police station?"

"Your place," Monique told him, then hoped she

had made the right choice. Because whether it was about protection or not, she knew that spending the night with Khamil would be far from uncomplicated.

Twelve

The moment Monique and Khamil stepped into the lobby of Khamil's upper west side condo, Monique's heart went berserk. All she could think of was how many other women had been to his place, how many had spent the night.

What was she doing here?

Khamil placed a hand on the small of her back and led her to the elevators. When the elevator door opened, she swallowed.

A beautiful young black woman exited the elevator with a fluffy white poodle. "Hello, Khamil," she said, greeting him.

"Hello, Diane."

Monique threw a glance at Khamil, wanting to ask who the woman was, but bit her tongue. Instead she asked herself, since when she had become so . . . jealous. Yes, she realized with chagrin, she *was* jealous. Maybe Khamil had been right when he'd said that she wanted him to give only her his attention.

But why? She didn't want a relationship with him.

She'd never been like this with anyone else. Even when Raymond had cheated on her, she'd simply told him it was over without a second thought. So why did who Khamil slept with matter to her one bit?

Khamil led Monique onto the elevator. He hit the button for the fifth floor. Moments later, the elevator came to a stop, and the doors opened.

Khamil started off the elevator, but Monique didn't move. Realizing she wasn't going anywhere, he paused, then faced her. "What's the matter?"

"I can't do this," Monique whispered.

"Can't do what?"

"What's up with you and Vicky?" Monique asked before she could stop herself.

"Me and Vicky?"

Monique angled her head to the side as she leveled her gaze at his face. "Yes, you and Vicky." Having seen them together in an embrace had been bothering her all evening, and she finally had the courage to ask him about the nature of their relationship. "Has she been here? To your place?"

"What are you talking about?"

To her own ears, she sounded ridiculous. Yet she continued. "You and Vicky seemed very *chummy* earlier. In fact, Vicky gave me some attitude when she questioned me about you, so . . ." Monique paused. "So, if there's something going on between the two of you, tell me now. Because I have to work with Vicky, and I don't want any unnecessary animosity between us."

Khamil let the elevator door close, then hit the stop button.

Monique's eyes bulged as she looked at him. "W-why are you—"

Khamil closed the distance between them and swept Monique into his arms. Without hesitation, he brought his lips down on hers—hard—swallowing Monique's moan of protest. Damn, she felt good. She was like an intoxicating drug, one he needed more and more of. Yet only kissing her wasn't enough.

He wanted all of her.

And he was tempted to take her, right here and now, and probably would have, if Monique hadn't slipped her hands between their bodies and pushed him away. As she stared up at him from lowered lashes, her chest rose and fell quickly with each breath she took.

"Does that answer your question?" Khamil asked.

Monique looked away. "Th-this is exactly what I-I don't want . . ."

"I think it's what you *do* want." When Monique's eyes flew to his, Khamil raised one eyebrow in challenge. "Otherwise, you wouldn't care less what was up with me and Vicky."

Monique's heart thumped hard in her chest. "So there *is* something between you and Vicky?"

"No, there isn't."

"Then why did she act like I was encroaching on her territory?"

"You'll have to ask her that."

It was suddenly hot in the elevator. Too hot. She believed Khamil, which surprised her, because a part of her had wanted to cling to the possibility that he was involved with someone else—anyone else—if for no other reason than to give herself an excuse to stay away from him. But there was something about Khamil that had her forgetting why getting involved with him would be wrong, and instead had her wishing that he'd take her in his arms and kiss her silly again.

Monique had to stop thinking like that. She hit the button to start the elevator. Then she pressed the button for the main level.

As the elevator started to move, Khamil hit the

stop button again. Once again, Monique's heart beat anxiously in her chest. She was both excited and alarmed at being trapped in an elevator with Khamil.

"You're not going back home, Monique."

She swallowed as her body shivered from the intensity of his words. "Fine," she told him. "I'll find my way to the nearest hotel."

"You are not staying at a hotel."

"Oh, yeah?" Monique said. "Try and stop me."

"I will, if that's what it takes."

Her eyes were wide with indignation, but Khamil held her gaze, letting her know he was not going to back down. He was crazy, but he wanted her. Wanted to take her in his arms and tear the form-fitting black pants and black tank top off her body. Wanted to take her wildly, right here on the elevator floor.

"Fine," Monique huffed, but Khamil got the feeling it was all for show. Then she started up the elevator again. "But first thing in the morning, I'm gone."

We'll see about that, Khamil thought, the edges of his lips curling in the slightest of smiles.

God help her, Monique was losing it! What was it about Khamil that made her angry one minute, then hot and bothered the next?

"Monique, do I need to invite you in?"

She was standing in the doorway of his apartment, but hadn't even realized it. Holding her head high, she strolled over the threshold.

"It's beautiful," Monique said, meaning it. She surveyed the small but quaint, modernly decorated condominium. Bright white walls contrasted with the black lacquer coffee table, the black and brass lamps, and the black leather sofa. Instantly, her mind started conjuring up ideas of how to add to the living room's appeal. Perhaps an area rug that added a splash of color, some classic paintings on the walls that mixed an old flavor with the modern.

Monique walked farther into the apartment. At the far end of the living room was a glass solarium. In the solarium, there was a beautiful glass dining table with black and brass trimmings. Two white candles rested on either end of the table in brass candleholders, complemented by a floral centerpiece.

The candles made Monique think of romance, and she couldn't help wondering how many romantic evenings Khamil had spent here . . .

Monique inhaled a steady breath, deliberately ignoring the direction of her thoughts. Retracing her steps through the living room, she went to the hallway. As she further explored the apartment, she discovered there was only one bedroom.

"Can I get you anything to drink?"

Startled at his voice, Monique spun around to find Khamil standing behind her. Maybe it was because she was at his bedroom door, but illicit thoughts crept into her mind, and she couldn't help throwing a glance over his entire body. Her gaze lingered on his thighs, which looked large and powerful beneath his black pants.

Oh, how she'd love to reach out and touch someone. . . .

"Monique?"

Her eyes flew to his face, embarrassed that he'd caught her staring. "Uh . . . sorry. What did you say?"

"I asked if you wanted a drink."

"A drink," Monique repeated, as though she didn't know the meaning of the word. Drinking and Khamil would not mix, not here at his place, when she couldn't stop noticing just how devastatingly sexy he was. "Uh, no." She forced a yawn. "I'm starting to drift. You know, get all blurry-eyed. I'd just like to go to bed."

His eyes held hers a moment too long, but she wouldn't look away. Couldn't. "I understand," he finally said. "The bed's all yours."

"Oh, no," Monique replied. There was no way she'd sleep in Khamil's bed. "I'll be fine on the couch." To prove her point, she walked back into the living room and sank into the softness of the black leather sofa.

Khamil followed her. "Monique." His voice was deep and oh-so sexy. Just the way he said her name made her skin tingle. "You get the bed. No arguments."

"No." Khamil's bed was too . . . personal. Sleeping in it would be crossing some sort of line. She brought her feet up to the couch and stretched out. "Just bring me a blanket and I'm good to go."

"The bed sheets are clean. I changed them this morning."

"Khamil—"

"You're taking the bed, Monique."

A small frown played on Monique's lips. "Do you always have to have your own way?"

"I'm trying to be a gentleman."

She flashed a plastic smile. "Offer appreciated. Declined."

"Suit yourself." His hands went to the front of his shirt and started undoing the buttons—slowly.

"*What* are you doing?"

"I'm sleeping on the couch, Monique. You're my guest. You get the bed."

"But you're too tall. You'll get a kink in your neck sleeping on the couch."

"I'll be all right." He pulled the shirt off his body.

Monique had forgotten just how sexy Khamil had looked without a shirt on the night of the charity fashion show, and now her breath snagged in her throat at the sight of his beautifully sculpted arms and smooth, dark chest. Damn, but this man was *fine*.

What was wrong with her? Only teenage women gawked at men the way she was gawking, didn't they?

Her mind returned to the dilemma at hand when she heard Khamil unzip his pants. "Hold up, Khamil," she said, throwing out a hand to stop him. She didn't want to see the rest of his magnificent body. She'd never maintain control of her raging hormones if he dropped his pants.

"Do I get the couch?" he asked, a sexy smile playing on his lips.

"Yes." She leaped off the couch. She'd agree to anything just to get away from him.

"Do you need a shirt to sleep in?"

She shook her head. "I've got nightwear in my overnight bag, thank you."

That shouldn't have excited him, but it did. Hell, it did. She'd look sexy in anything, but he wondered what she preferred to wear to bed. Sexy teddies, or a simple T-shirt? He wouldn't mind seeing her in one of his plaid shirts, unbuttoned to her cleavage.

"I'll just go to . . . bed now."

"Okay," Khamil replied. "See you in the morning."

"Good night." Monique made a hasty retreat, grabbing her overnight bag along the way. When she closed the bedroom door behind her, she laid her forehead against it for several seconds.

Goodness, Khamil was hot! And so was she, just thinking about his hard, muscular chest, his smooth, dark brown skin, his firm butt, and those sexy thighs . . . She sucked in a sharp breath and let it out slowly. The scent of him filled her senses. She couldn't sleep in his room. In his *bed*. She would call a cab and go to a hotel.

She reached for the doorknob, then stopped. This was crazy. *She* was crazy. If she left, he'd chase her. Her heart thumped at the thought. Gosh, she really was crazy. She actually liked the idea of Khamil chasing her, that he didn't want her to leave . . .

There was a knock at the door. "Monique."

She froze.

"Monique," he repeated softly.

"Y—yes?"

"I'm going to use the bathroom. Give me five minutes; then it's all yours."

"Okay." She waited, wondering if Khamil was going to open the door. *Wanting* him to. But all she heard was the soft sound of his footsteps as he walked away.

Frustrated, she sighed. This was going to be one *long* night.

Thirteen

Khamil couldn't sleep. There was no point even trying. The knowledge that Monique lay in his bed, just down the hallway, consumed his thoughts.

What would she be like in bed? Would she be wild, digging her nails into his back and calling out his name? Or was she the quiet but intense type?

The irony of the situation wasn't lost on him. He rarely had a woman in his apartment if she wasn't sharing his bed. And despite the fact that Monique wasn't here to be his lover, he wanted her. Wanted to press himself against her curves, sink his body into her soft, hot spot.

"Cool it, Khamil," he told himself. He closed his eyes and started counting sheep, hoping that would take his mind off the woman in his bed.

Monique couldn't sleep. Groaning, she rolled over onto her side and buried her face in the pillow. Then she rolled over again.

This was pointless. At most, she'd had a few precious minutes of sleep here and there throughout the night. And now, sunlight spilled through the blinds, overpowering the darkness.

Fresh sheets may have been on the bed, but

Khamil's scent was everywhere. Surrounding her, invading her senses.

Khamil . . . It was hard not to imagine him in the bed with her. Hard not to imagine how his gaze alone had made her shudder with longing. Hard not to remember the rush of excitement she'd felt when he'd pulled her to him in the elevator, crushing her breasts against his solid chest.

Her eyes flew open. Was that a sound she heard outside her room? Heart pounding, she swallowed and waited.

Nothing.

Chiding herself for feeling disappointed, she rolled onto her side. Something caught her eye.

She screamed.

He'd just drifted to sleep when the bloodcurdling cry bolted him awake. *Monique.* Scrambling from the sofa, Khamil darted to the bedroom. Threw open the door.

Stopped dead in his tracks.

"Khamil!" Monique cried, relief evident in her bulging eyes. "Oh, God, it's there. Right *there.*"

He could hardly concentrate on what she was saying. Standing by the window, she wore only some scrap of ivory on her skin. Ivory lace. God, he was lost.

"Khamil! You have to do *something!*"

"W-what is it?"

"I don't know. Just kill it!"

Khamil ventured farther into the room, his eyes darting to the spot where Monique was pointing. When he saw the object of her fear, he shook his head. "This is why you screamed bloody murder?"

"Kill it. Khamil, please kill it." With each word, she backed farther away.

"It's only a bug."

"It's god-awful ugly, that's what it is! Ew! Look at all those legs. It's disgusting. And I've never seen anything that big in my life. Good grief, you should charge it rent!"

Khamil looked at the offending bug, which was on the wall beside the bed. Monique was right. It was ugly. He wasn't sure if it was a centipede or what, but it had about a gazillion legs and was probably two inches long.

He took a step forward. Monique jumped. He looked at her closely. She was shivering. God, she was really afraid. He suddenly wanted to comfort her, make the fear go away. "Don't worry. I'll get rid of it."

Khamil grabbed a Kleenex from the box on the night table, then rounded the side of the bed to get near the bug. Moving slowly, he covered the creature with the Kleenex, skillfully capturing it without killing it.

"I'll be right back."

Monique let out a sigh of relief as Khamil left the room, then immediately felt like a fool. If she could take this all back, she would. Screaming at the sight of a bug! It was absolutely absurd.

She could handle spiders, lizards, snakes even, but not that horribly disgusting bug that looked about a foot long.

Moments later, Khamil returned. "It's gone."

"Where?"

"I opened a window and let it outside."

She'd been too absorbed in the bug drama to notice what Khamil was wearing—or rather, *not* wearing. White cotton boxers covered the bare essentials—

barely. Through his pants, it was clear Khamil's legs were muscular, but naked—he was perfect. Every part of his body was taut with beautiful muscles.

He was walking toward her. Monique's body stiffened, but she was helpless to move. Her eyes caught his, held his gaze.

It seemed like an eternity before he reached her.

"Khamil—"

"Monique—"

They spoke at the same time.

"Go ahead," she said, surprised to find her voice was barely a whisper.

He opened his mouth to speak. Closed it. Stared at her.

Her lips suddenly felt very dry and she flicked her tongue out to wet them. Immediately, she saw the response in Khamil's eyes. They darkened. Narrowed. She licked her lips again.

"Don't . . . do that."

Deliberately, she ran her tongue over her bottom lip. "This?" she asked innocently. She was teasing him, tempting him, and she didn't know why.

"Yes, that."

Something passed between them, something electrifying, exciting. He was so close now his breath fanned her forehead. In the silence of the room, she was sure she could hear her blood flowing through her veins.

He reached out and captured her wrist, stroking the inside with his thumb. The simple action made her heart pound furiously.

"Unresolved," he muttered.

"Hmm?" All she had to do was stand on her toes and her lips would brush against his.

"Ever since the first night I met you, I've wanted you. I think you feel the same way." Khamil gently stroked the smooth skin of Monique's face. She quivered at his touch. "God, Monique, I love the way you respond to my touch. It makes me hot."

Monique's throat constricted, preventing any words from escaping. She was completely distracted by Khamil's touch, by his words, by his heated gaze.

"We've been skirting around the issue," Khamil said, his voice husky. "But it's clear we want each other. There's so much tension between us . . ."

Before she knew what was happening, Khamil tilted her chin upward and lowered his lips to meet hers, surprising her with a delicate kiss. His mouth was as soft as velvet and lingered on hers, gently parting her lips with his tongue. He reached for her face with both hands, cupping it tenderly. His tongue was warm as it danced with her own, teasing her, exciting her beyond anything she could ever have imagined.

The kiss sent a tingling sensation all through Monique's body, electrifying and awakening every cell. When Khamil finally pulled his head away from hers to catch his breath, Monique felt as though someone had doused her with a glass of cold water. She hungered for more of what she had just experienced.

"You are the most beautiful woman I have ever laid my eyes on." Cupping Monique's chin, Khamil smiled down at her, a genuine, dazzling smile. Monique stared back at him in stunned silence.

"I want to make love to you."

"Khamil. . . ." His name escaped on a breathless sigh.

"That's it, Monique. Let me know how much you want me." He trailed a finger from her neck to one soft mound of her breast.

"I want you," she said softly, surprised at her words.

Khamil covered her lips with his and wrapped his arms around her. Knowing that there was no turning back now, Monique wrapped her arms tightly around his neck.

And she didn't want to turn back.

"I want you so much," Khamil whispered against her ear as he urged her back onto his bed.

And then he was kissing her again, slowly at first, teasing her. But then his warm, wet tongue delved into her mouth with urgency, and the kiss became an explosion of desire.

Monique surrendered to the kiss, to the blinding desire that consumed her. Her tongue danced with Khamil's in a desperate song of passion. His mouth was warm and sweet and intoxicating. She moaned against his kiss, enjoying the here and now, not thinking about tomorrow.

Breaking the kiss, Khamil looked deeply into Monique's eyes. "Are you sure?"

Bereft of speech, Monique nodded.

Khamil's eyes crinkled as he looked down at her, heated longing evident in their depths. He brought his hand to her lips and softly traced the outline of her mouth with one finger. One finger, yet the light touch was so stimulating, Monique's entire body tingled with sexual fervor.

With his skilled hands, Khamil trailed a sensuous path down her smooth neck, then pulled the string that the held the front of her lacy camisole together. The camisole loosened, and Khamil spread the material apart, exposing her breasts. He groaned softly, then brought his tongue to her searing skin and kissed the smooth, soft flesh between her breasts. Monique shuddered with delight as Khamil ran his tongue along her skin, up to the hollow of her neck, and back down again.

"You're so beautiful," he said softly. Bringing both hands to her breasts, he stroked and kneaded the supple flesh. Then, he lowered his head and circled his tongue around a hard peak. Thrilled with the glorious feel of his tongue, Monique arched her back seductively, wanting more. She moaned Khamil's name when he took her nipple completely into his mouth.

Fire soared through Monique's veins right to her feminine core. Wantonly, she clasped Khamil's head, holding it to her breast as he suckled, as ripples of pleasure coursed through her body.

She was mad with sweet longing, unlike anything she had ever experienced. Both hot and wet, her center of pleasure was throbbing incessantly. And just when she thought she would die of the ecstasy, Khamil slid a hand beneath her camisole and began daintily caressing her most private part. A rapturous moan escaped Monique's lips, and between ragged breaths she said, "Oh, Khamil. I need you."

Monique pulled herself up onto her side and reached for Khamil's boxers. Her fingers were shaking as she tugged at them. Khamil eased himself up, allowing her to slip the boxers over his hips. Hastily, Monique dragged them down the length of his muscular legs.

Khamil pulled her to him. A sliver of desire skittered down Monique's spine as her hardened nipples grazed the solid muscles of Khamil's chest. She brought her mouth to his neck and ran her tongue along it, wanting to excite Khamil the way he was exciting her. Khamil gripped her arms, a raw sexual groan emanating from his throat. Feeling a sudden surge of power, Monique skimmed her tongue down to his chest, across the heated, brawny flesh, then over to one of his small nipples, taking the peak between her teeth.

Khamil shuddered, then pushed Monique onto her back with a force that thrilled her. She stared up at him from lowered lids, and watched as he brought his hand to her breast, gliding his fingers along the full, soft flesh. He reached for the camisole, and Monique moved her body, allowing him to take it off.

Khamil's breath caught in his throat as he took in Monique's exquisite beauty. Her firm, flat stomach, her slim waist, her full, soft breasts and their dark, erect tips. "You're perfect, Monique," he uttered softly. "Absolutely beautiful." He lay beside her and kissed her lightly, then with his fingers trailed a fiery path from her neck to her stomach, stopping just above her lace panties.

"Don't stop," Monique said, stroking his face. "Make love to me."

With delicate hands, Khamil skimmed the white lace panties over Monique's round hips, then over her long, smooth legs. An inferno of passion was burning in his loins as his eyes roamed her body, her silky, dark skin and tempting curves.

His gaze holding hers, Khamil lowered himself onto Monique's body, gently parting her legs with his own. Slipping a hand between their bodies, he found her throbbing center, then moaned softly when he discovered she was wet and ready for him. He immersed a finger deep inside her, enjoying the way she arched her back at his touch, the way an excited moan escaped her lips. He played with her until she was whimpering and groaning and tossing her head from side to side, until he could no longer stand not being inside her.

"Just a second." Easing himself off the bed,

Khamil reached for the top drawer on the night table. He pulled out a condom, tore open the package, then put the condom on.

Monique still lay ready for him, and he settled himself between her legs. Then, capturing her mouth with his, he entered her.

A half moan, half cry fell from Monique's lips. She dug her nails into Khamil's back, squeezing hard as he thrust deep inside her. Nothing had ever felt as glorious as this. Her body was alive with sensations, wonderful sensations that threatened to take control of her very being. "Oh, yes!" she cried. "Oh, Khamil. . . ."

Monique was driving him crazy. She knew just how to touch him, how to meet his wild thrusts. It was as if they were familiar with each other's bodies, with what thrilled and turned each other on. Yet they were lovers for the first time.

"Khamil!" Monique squealed, gripping his firm buttocks as the most delightful dizzying sensation swept over her. She let out a loud, ravished moan as her hips bucked savagely, as contractions rippled through her core, one after the other until every ounce of strength drained from her body. As the contractions subsided, she clung to Khamil's slick body, luxuriating in the aftermath of her splendid climax, knowing that what she had just experienced was heaven on earth. She wished she could stay in his arms forever.

Khamil seized Monique's lips in a short, fierce kiss, just before his head grew light and his body grew taut. He plunged into Monique's sweet warmth one last time, collapsing on top of her as he succumbed to his glorious release. As sweet sensations rocked his body, he held her to him tightly, knowing that he had never experienced anything quite as wonderful as this with any other woman.

They stayed there like that, holding each other, their bodies wet, their breathing frantic. And finally, when their breathing returned to normal, Khamil slid off Monique and lay beside her.

"My God, Monique." Khamil kissed her temple as he wrapped an arm over her waist. "What have you done to me?"

Monique turned in Khamil's arms, surprisingly content. Their lovemaking had been explosive, and there was no point denying that. "The same thing you've done to me."

Silence fell between them as they snuggled up together.

"Maybe now I can finally get some sleep," Khamil whispered.

Monique chuckled softly. "Me, too."

Khamil pulled her closer, and Monique closed her eyes. Yeah, she'd sleep well. At least for a while.

Fourteen

The sound of Monique's beeper going off jarred her from sleep. For a moment she was stunned to find herself in a strange bed. But the strong arms around her instantly reminded her of where she was.

In Khamil's bed.

Khamil stirred. "What was that?"

"My beeper," Monique answered. She glanced at the digital clock on Khamil's night table. It was thirteen minutes after nine. "That's probably my agent."

Monique moved to the side of the bed and reached for her purse on the floor. She dug out her beeper and checked the number. As she'd thought, it was her agent's number. Her family also had her beeper number, but were instructed to use it only if there was a dire emergency. Thus far, that hadn't happened.

"Yeah, it's my agent," Monique said.

"You need to use the phone?" Khamil asked.

"Yeah. I'll go to the living room."

"No, go ahead and use this phone. I need to get up anyway."

Khamil threw the covers off his body and climbed from the bed, naked as the day he was born. Monique couldn't help checking out his firm butt as he walked to the closet. Seconds later, he slipped into a terry-cloth robe.

The sight of his naked body was an all too real reminder of what had happened last night. As Khamil exited the bedroom, Monique wondered what today would bring. Was last night simply a one-time deal? And did she want any more than that? Between her modeling career and her quest to find her mother's killer, she wasn't sure she had much to offer a man in a relationship.

Putting those thoughts out of her mind, she reached for the phone and dialed her agent. Kelly, the receptionist, answered.

"Morning, Kelly. It's Monique Savard. Is Elaine in?"

"Yep. One second."

A moment later, Elaine said, "Elaine Cox."

"Hello, Elaine. It's Monique."

"Hi, Monique." She paused. "Listen. There was a message for you on the office voice mail this morning."

"Really?" Who would leave a message for her at her agency, rather than at her home number?

"Yeah. And it's kind of cryptic, but sounded important, so I figured I'd call you right away with it."

Monique sat up. "Okay."

"The person's voice sounded muffled, so I couldn't make out if it was a man or a woman. But the message said that you should check the house in Canada, that she probably kept the letters. They will give you the answers you're looking for."

"What?" Monique asked, more out of confusion than because she hadn't heard what Elaine had said.

Elaine repeated the message, then said, "Hopefully, you know what the heck that means."

"I think so," Monique answered, though she really

had no clue. But more baffling than the cryptic message was the issue as to who had called her agent. "And this person didn't leave a name, or a number where I could reach them?"

"Nope. Sorry." Elaine paused, then asked, "Is this about your mother?"

"I'm sure it is." That had to be the "she" the mysterious caller had referred to. Confused, Monique blew out a frazzled breath. What letters? And what kind of clue did they hold as to the identity of her mother's murderer?

There was only one thing she was sure of. If there was some type of lead at her family's cottage in Canada, then she had to go check it out. Immediately. "Look, Elaine. I'm gonna head out of town for a few days, but I'll be back in time for the Cover Girl shoot next week."

"Monique." Elaine's tone was wary. "I'm worried about you."

"I'll be fine," she told her. "But this is something I have to do."

"Please be careful."

"I will."

"And call me with a number where I can reach you."

"All right. I will. Thanks for giving me the message."

"Of course."

"I'll talk to you later," Monique said, then replaced the receiver. She pulled her legs to her chest, her mind trying to make sense of the information she'd just received.

What was going on? Who had called? Someone who'd seen *America's Most Wanted* and was calling with a tip? And if so, why hadn't they called the police?

The knock at the door interrupted her thoughts.

Monique adjusted the blanket over her breasts, then said, "Come in."

As if he sensed something was bothering her, Khamil looked at her with concern. "Everything okay?"

"I don't know."

"What do you mean you don't know?"

"I got a weird call from my agent," Monique explained. "Someone called and left a message for me to check the house in Canada because there'll be answers there. They mentioned some letters."

"You still have the house?"

Monique met Khamil's eyes. "Yeah."

"Then whoever called is someone you know."

A chill slithered down Monique's spine.

"Otherwise, why would they tell you to check the house? If it was someone you didn't know, they wouldn't know if you still had the house. Hell, they wouldn't know about any letters."

"You're right." At first, Monique had wondered if the call had possibly been a prank. But Khamil was right. If someone knew her family still had the house, then there was no way the message could be a prank.

Still covering herself with the bedsheet, Monique reached for one of Khamil's shirts, which hung on a bedpost. She slipped it on. Then she stood and reached for her overnight bag.

Khamil walked farther into the room. "What are you doing?"

"I have to go." Monique reached into the bag and pulled out her bra and a clean pair of underwear.

"Where?" Khamil asked, his tone wary.

"I have to go to Canada."

"Wait a second." Khamil stopped before her. "You

get a weird call about some clue and you're just gonna get up and take off to Canada?"

"I have to, Khamil." Monique slipped the underwear on. "If there are answers there, I need to find them."

"Fine, I hear you. But you can't just get up and go."

"Why not?"

Khamil shook his head with dismay as he stared at Monique. She didn't look at him as she slipped her bra around her waist, fastened it, then pulled it over her breasts. Last night, they'd spent an incredible night making love, and now, she was ready to run off as if nothing had happened between them.

"Don't you want to have a shower?"

"I can have one at home."

Khamil couldn't help feeling a sense of disappointment as he watched Monique slip into her pants. "And last night . . ."

"I don't have time to talk about that right now."

"I see." Turning, Khamil walked toward the bedroom door. He didn't know what to make of Monique. Last night, she'd been concerned that he was involved with someone else, making it seem as though she may have wanted more from him. Now, she was acting as if she didn't give a damn about him in any way, not even the fact that they'd made love.

Khamil faced Monique again. She was now fully dressed. "Are you going to the police?"

"Yeah, I'll go. After I head home and make my travel arrangements."

Monique returned Khamil's shirt to the bedpost, then took one last look around. Satisfied that she had everything, she headed for the bedroom door.

"All right," she said, stopping before Khamil. "I'll call you later."

She stepped past him, but Khamil took hold of her arm, stopping her. "That's it? You spend the night with me, and you leave?"

"I'm sorry, Khamil." Monique ran her free hand over her hair. "I've got a lot on my mind."

"Fine," Khamil conceded. "Will you call me when you get there?"

Monique nodded. "Sure."

Khamil didn't like this. He didn't like Monique's indifferent attitude toward him, and he sure didn't like the idea of her chasing some lead about a murder by herself. "Be careful," he told her.

"I will."

Lowering his head, Khamil surprised Monique with a soft kiss on the lips. Even though the contact was brief, she savored the feel and taste of him. Glancing into his eyes, she saw sincerity in their dark brown depths, and butterflies danced in her stomach.

Last night with Khamil had been nothing short of wonderful. He was a skilled lover, but she'd known he would be. He seemed sincere enough, and had been good to her, yet she wasn't sure she was ready to consider anything more than last night. For one, Khamil hadn't said he wanted anything more. And until her own life's messes were straightened out, she didn't know if she'd truly be able to give her heart to anybody.

Yet she couldn't deny they'd shared something special. Reaching for his face, she palmed one of his cheeks. "I have to go."

Khamil turned his face in her hand so that his lips met her palm. He gave her hand a brief kiss. "Please call me later."

"I will," Monique promised.

* * *

Khamil had already called the office the night before to let them know he'd be working from home today. But he was completely unable to concentrate on the contracts that lay before him on his dining room table.

All he could think about was Monique, and what kind of trouble she might be getting herself into.

He was worried about her.

He'd called her apartment once already, but she hadn't answered her phone. No doubt, she was at the police station. That thought should have given him comfort, but it didn't. There were way too many cases in which the police didn't and couldn't do anything about an anonymous threat until it was too late.

Standing, Khamil gathered the loose files from the table and dropped them into his briefcase. If he stayed at home and worked and anything happened to Monique, he'd never forgive himself.

Javar had had a premonition the night their mother had tried to murder Whitney, and that premonition had brought him to his wife's side in the nick of time. And one night long ago, during college, Khamil had had a premonition that had saved his life. He'd refused to go out after a football game with two other players from the team who were heading across the border to Windsor, Canada, for a night of clubbing. Eric and Trey had been hit by an out-of-control truck that had crossed the median en route to the Canadian border, and both were killed instantly. Their car had been a mass of crushed fiberglass and metal; Eric and Trey hadn't stood a chance.

If Khamil had gone with them, there was no doubt he would have been killed as well.

He believed in instincts, believed in trusting them. As a lawyer, he had to—and they never steered him wrong.

Right now, Khamil's instincts told him that Monique needed him. And they were too strong to ignore.

His briefcase closed, Khamil quickly headed to the bedroom to dress, hoping he wasn't too late to reach Monique before she left for Canada.

Having called her travel agent on the way home and learning that there weren't any flights for Toronto until the afternoon, Monique had decided to do as Khamil had suggested and went to the police station to report the threatening letters she'd received. As she'd guessed, there wasn't much the police could do about the letters, except open a file for her case.

"If you get anything else, let us know," the officer she'd dealt with had told her.

Now, Monique sat in the back of a taxi, heading home where she would pack. She still had four hours before her flight from JFK, but already she was anxious. What kind of clue could be in the house? And who would know about it? Surely if her father knew about the clue he would have brought this to the police's attention years ago.

Unless it was something that would further implicate him in the crime.

For the second time, she allowed herself to consider what Doreen always tried to impress upon her. There *was* a possibility that her father could have killed her mother.

That was nonsense, Monique concluded almost as quickly as the thought had formed. Deep in her heart, she knew that her father didn't have anything to do with her mother's death. Still, it was obvious that someone knew something, and the fact that that someone knew her family still owned the house in Canada deeply disturbed her.

It had to be someone close to her.

But who?

Or, she suddenly realized, it could be someone who still lived in the neighborhood where they'd had their summer home. Yes, she thought, a wave of relief washing over her, that made sense. A neighbor might know that the house had never been sold, and may even know something that had happened that horrible night. For whatever reason, this person may have been scared to come forward—until now.

That thought comforted her, even though she was no closer to having any answers. Bottom line, she didn't want to think that anyone close to the family might have known and withheld vital information about her mother's murder from the police.

The taxi pulled to a stop in front of her building. She paid the driver as Harry opened the door. She smiled at Harry, but her smile quickly faded as she looked past his shoulder and saw Khamil standing near the building's front door.

"You have a guest," Harry told her.

"Yes," Monique said absently. "I see."

Monique headed toward Khamil, noting the brief-case and small piece of luggage at his feet. "Khamil, what are you doing?"

"I'm going with you," he replied simply.

Monique narrowed her eyes as she looked at him. "Going with me where?"

"To Toronto."

"Toronto?" She gaped at him. "What on earth for?"

Khamil replied, "I have business up there."

"Really?" Monique sounded skeptical.

"Toronto has a booming entertainment industry. Many talent from there work on both sides of the border, and vice versa. In fact, a New York producer is up there filming a feature right now, and he needs me to look over a contract for one of the secondary characters who wants to do some negotiating. So I have plenty to do."

Monique's expression said she didn't believe him.

"And," Khamil continued, "I don't want you to go alone."

"Khamil . . ."

"Don't bother telling me to go home. The man who killed your mother is still on the loose. There's no way I'm going to let you put yourself at risk."

Monique felt a little jolt in her heart at his words, and her entire body got warm. God help her, his stubbornness turned her on. "Why not?"

"We're friends. I'm always there for my friends."

Disappointment bubbled in Monique's stomach at Khamil's description of their relationship. Yet that's all they were—friends who had shared a passionate night of lovemaking.

"I'm sure you have better things to do than baby-sit me," Monique told him.

Khamil lifted the briefcase. "I've got work in here. I've got my cell phone. I'm good to go."

Monique blew out a sigh. The idea of having company on this trip made her feel much better. "All right. If you're sure."

"I am."

"Well, I still have to pack," Monique explained,

stepping into the building as Harry held the door open for her. She passed him a few bills. "I went to the police station, but like I thought, there's not much they can do."

"You filed a report, right?"

"Uh-huh. So, we'll see." Monique hit the elevator button. "But I'm not about to wait around for the police to do anything. Do you know how many times my mother reported the threats she'd been receiving? In the end, it didn't do her any good."

The elevator doors opened. A couple exited, and then Monique and Khamil entered.

"I called about flights," Monique began when the door closed. "There's one that leaves JFK for Toronto at three fifty-five this afternoon."

"Cool. That'll give us time to stop to get something to eat before we head to the airport."

The elevator made a soft pinging sound as it landed on the penthouse floor. The doors opened and Monique made her way off the elevator, followed by Khamil.

They walked in silence down the hallway, Monique reaching into her purse for her keys. At her apartment door, Monique tried inserting the key, but it wouldn't go in.

Holding up the key chain, Monique sorted through the keys until she found another similar one. She often confused the two keys. She placed the second key into the slot and pushed, but like the first one, it wouldn't go in, either.

"Having trouble?" Khamil asked, his breath warm on Monique's neck.

Monique's eyes fluttered shut as Khamil's breath tickled her neck. "No," she replied as calmly as she could.

"It looks like you're having trouble to me,"

Khamil said, putting his hand on hers. "Let me help."

With his slightly callused hand resting delicately on hers, Khamil helped her insert the key in the lock. You'd think he was slowly disrobing her, the way Monique's body got excited at Khamil's touch.

And that was the problem, she realized. With Khamil around, she didn't focus on what was important because she couldn't seem to keep her raging hormones under control around him. Right now, she should be concerned with whatever clue might be at the cottage in Canada, not with how wonderful it had felt to be in Khamil's arms last night.

"This is the key?" Khamil asked.

"I think so," Monique replied.

Khamil's fingers wrapped around hers. He tried to turn the key, but it wouldn't move. "Wait a second," he said. He wiggled the key in the lock. "That's strange. It won't go all the way in."

Monique's gaze fell to the key. Khamil was right. Maybe she'd messed up with the first key. "Try the other silver key."

Khamil tried the second silver key, but again, it didn't insert completely into the lock. He withdrew the key and bent his head to inspect the lock closer. Then his eyes flew to Monique's, panic written on his face.

"What?" Monique asked. She hugged her torso, suddenly feeling cold.

"It looks like someone tampered with the lock."

"What?"

"The edges of the slot are bent slightly. Damaged. See?"

Monique looked where Khamil indicated. Then she nodded, acknowledging that he was right.

"Almost as if someone took a screwdriver to it or something."

Something made Monique reach for the door handle and turn it. And when it opened, she threw a worried glance at Khamil. She never left her apartment door unlocked.

Khamil saw the concern in Monique's eyes and matched it with a look of his own. After a moment, he put a finger to his mouth, indicating for Monique to be quiet.

Then he silently edged open the door and stepped into the apartment.

Fifteen

Monique's heart pounded as she watched Khamil creep into her apartment. She was so frightened, she couldn't move.

"Oh, God," Khamil said.

"What?" Monique's stomach lurched with fear.

"Damn." Khamil turned to face her. "Someone's definitely been in here, Monique."

Hearing Khamil's words, she felt a shiver pass over her body. Yet she'd known that had to be the case the moment she discovered the apartment was open. As much as she'd wanted to believe she could have accidentally left the door unlocked, she knew that wasn't likely.

As Khamil continued to stare at her, Monique slowly entered her penthouse unit. A startled cry fell from her mouth at what she saw.

On the wall, written in red, was the word *Whore.*

And all over the floor, there were red rose petals. The petals had not only been ripped from their buds, many had been crushed into her carpet with someone's shoe heel.

Monique closed her eyes tightly as panic swept over her. "Oh, my God."

Khamil placed both hands on Monique's shoulders, and she opened her eyes to find him staring at her intensely. "Monique." Khamil pressed his fingers into her shoulders softly, but firmly. "Do you have *any* idea who could have done this?"

She thought a moment, then said, "Raymond."

"Raymond?"

"The guy who was at Angel's that night," Monique explained. "When I kissed you. He's the only one who had a key."

Khamil stood straight, his hands falling to his sides. "He had a key to your place?"

Monique nodded.

"So the relationship was serious."

"I guess," Monique said. "I trusted him. But then he started acting crazy. He cheated on me, so I broke up with him. But then he wanted me back."

Khamil's eyebrows shot together. "How crazy? Crazy enough to be the person behind the threats?"

Monique blew out a hurried breath as she contemplated the thought. "Maybe. And he *does* know where I live. He knows my agency. He works a lot of the models' shoots."

One of Khamil's eyebrows shot up. "He does?"

"Yes." Oh, goodness. Could Raymond really be the one behind all of this? "He did make some weird comment about knowing something about my mother's death. At the time, I brushed that off as another lame attempt on his part to get me back, because he said he'd tell me what he knew if I got back together with him."

"And this guy still has a key to your place?" Khamil asked, his tone incredulous.

"Not because I want him to. He made a copy," Monique explained. "But when he showed up here the last time, I asked him for it. He gave it to me." Glancing at the floor, Monique frowned. "I suppose it's possible he had a few copies made." Her eyes wandered back up to Khamil's face. "But if he had a key, why break into the apartment?"

Khamil pursed his lips, contemplating the question. "Maybe he didn't break in," he said after a long moment. At Monique's confused expression, he added, "Maybe he opened the door, came in and did all this, then tampered with the lock afterward to make it *look* like a break-in." Khamil paused, his forehead furrowing. "And you said 'the last time.' When did he show up here?"

"A few weeks ago."

Alarm flashed in his eyes. "Did you call the police?"

"No. I asked for the key back, he gave it to me, and I thought that would be the end of it."

"Monique . . ."

"Fine, I made a mistake. I had no clue he'd be so . . . insane." Monique's bottom lip quivered as she glanced at the wall, then back at Khamil. "But what if it *wasn't* Raymond? What if it was someone else?" Hugging her torso, she turned away at the disturbing thought. "Oh, God."

"I'm calling the police," Khamil announced. "In the meantime, pack a suitcase. A large one. I don't want you coming back here."

When the police finished taking their statements, they promised they'd send a detective to talk to Raymond. In the meantime, they had retrieved the building's security tape to see who had gone in and out of the apartment in the last twenty-four hours.

Still shaken, Monique sat on her sofa, her elbows resting on her knees, her chin resting in her palms.

"You still want to go?" Khamil asked.

Monique looked up at him, knowing he meant

whether or not she still wanted to go to Canada. She nodded. "Yes. I have to."

Khamil lowered himself onto the sofa beside her. "This could simply be a coincidence. The person who sent you the letters referring to your mother might not be the person who did this. In fact, it makes perfect sense that it was Raymond who trashed your apartment, angry at you because he saw you with me."

Monique lowered her gaze to the cream-colored carpet. Her eyes caught a spot where the red roses had stained it. It looked like a spot of blood. . . .

"Help . . . me. . . ."

Monique squeezed her eyes tightly, trying to block out the haunting memory. But she couldn't. Her mother's blood had stained the carpet in the bedroom just as these red roses had stained hers.

Was this a coincidence? Or was the person who'd stalked and killed her mother toying with her?

Monique shot to her feet. "I need to get out of here."

"Monique."

Not wanting to fall apart in front of Khamil, Monique turned toward the window. A second later, she flinched when he wrapped his arms around her.

"It's okay, Monique," he said softly. "You don't have to be strong all the time. I know how hard this is for you."

"How do you know?" Monique asked. "How could you possibly know?"

"Because I've been through my own share of tragedies, Monique. My uncle was killed in the line of duty at a routine traffic stop in Chicago. Yes, his killer was caught, but the grief never quite goes away. And . . ." Khamil's voice trailed off. It was still hard for him to admit this to anyone, and very few people knew the truth. "My mother is behind bars for attempted murder."

Monique turned in his arms, staring at Khamil with curious eyes.

"It's a long story, and I'll tell it to you someday, but the gist of it is that my mother hated my brother's wife, and tried to kill her a couple times. The first time, she succeeded in killing my nephew— her own grandchild."

Monique threw a hand to her mouth. "Oh, Khamil. I'm so sorry."

"He was only five," Khamil went on. "Of course, my mother never expected him to be in the car she'd sabotaged in an effort to get rid of my sister-in-law, Whitney. My mother's actions tore our family apart, and ruined my brother's marriage for a couple years. Javar blamed Whitney for the accident, because Javar Junior hadn't been buckled in. And of course, you can imagine what kind of guilt my sister-in-law lived with. It wasn't until a couple years after my nephew's death that we learned the truth about the accident, that it wasn't Whitney's fault."

"How?" Monique asked.

"My mother tried to kill Whitney again. My mother's a doctor, and she'd drugged Whitney, with plans of drowning her in the lake."

Monique gasped.

"Yeah, I know. Anyway, to make a long story short, Javar got to her before it was too late, and my mother confessed to everything."

"Khamil, that's so horrible." She placed a hand on his forearm and gently stroked it. "Did your brother and his wife work things out?"

Khamil nodded. "Thankfully. And everything's fine now between them. They have three-year-old twins, and I just found out they're expecting another baby.''

A smile touched Monique's face. She loved happy endings. It was what she still hoped for in her mother's case. "Oh, that's wonderful."

"Yeah," Khamil said proudly. "But my mother . . . she's in prison, and she'll be there for a very long time."

"I'm sorry," Monique said. In a small way, it gave her comfort to know that she wasn't the only one who'd gone through something devastating, even though the kind of pain she'd suffered wasn't something she would wish on her worst enemy. But for the first time, she felt that someone not only cared, but understood.

"She did the crime, now she's doing the time," Khamil said, as though it was no big deal. But Monique could see the pain in his eyes.

"Do you talk to her?"

"My mother?"

Monique nodded.

"Not really. She still blames Whitney for everything that's happened, and to tell the truth, I can't deal with her."

"I see." Turning, Monique strolled to the window and peered down at the view of Central Park. It was a picturesque day, with a cloudless blue sky. What she'd give to be carefree and able to stroll through the park without any worries about anything.

Except, perhaps, falling in love.

Butterflies danced in Monique's stomach at the direction of her thoughts. *In love?* Why on earth had that come into her mind?

But she knew. Spinning around, she saw Khamil. He was staring at her, and his eyes met hers.

He was an enigma. Playful yet serious, cocky yet not full of himself . . . She was falling for the caring side she saw in him, despite the fact that his playful, cocky side made her wonder if he was a seasoned playboy.

What if he is? she asked herself. *Can't people change?*

Once again, she faced the window, the hope she'd felt a moment earlier fizzing. She was too old and had been in one too many relationships to delude herself with the wish that someone could change their ways. Once a player, always a player, as the saying went. While she had no doubt that Khamil was attracted to her, she seriously doubted if the attraction would last. There were no pictures of women in his apartment, indicating to her that none stayed in his life for any length of time.

Why should she be any different?

She wouldn't allow herself to get her hopes up, because that would only lead to disappointment. She would accept his friendship—because she needed a friend, and he seemed to understand her pain.

But she'd certainly make sure to guard her heart.

It seemed like days later that Khamil and Monique arrived at Pearson International Airport in Toronto, when in fact it had only been hours. Because of the break-in at her place and having to give reports to the police, they'd had to catch a later flight than planned. Now, it was evening in Toronto, and Monique had no desire to head an hour and a half north of the city to her family's cottage.

As if reading her thoughts, Khamil said, "It's late. Maybe we should get a hotel and get some rest, then get to work in the morning."

"I was thinking the same thing," Monique told him. "In fact, I'd meant to call my cousins and my father to let them know I'm here. I can do that from the hotel."

Their luggage in hand, Khamil and Monique headed outside the terminal. The first shuttle they saw was for the Holiday Inn, and they got on board.

Khamil placed his arm around Monique's shoulder as the bus started to move, and she rested her head against his shoulder. Glancing down at her, Khamil stroked her jet-black tresses.

He felt comfortable with Monique, more comfortable than he'd felt with any other woman he'd ever been with. Perhaps it was because she wasn't like the others. She was strong, independent, and she sure didn't act as if she needed him. Which, Khamil had discovered, was a quality that attracted him. It was exactly what he wanted. A woman who was self-sufficient, who didn't need a man for anything but wanted one for a satisfying relationship.

He frowned at the direction of his thoughts. Why was he thinking of a relationship? What they'd shared was sex, pure and simple. Besides, not only had Monique not made any mention of wanting anything more, she'd practically run from his bed and his apartment the morning after, seeming not to care about even the possibility of more with him.

Maybe that's what intrigued him. The chase. So many women these days did the chasing, taking away that traditional role from men. Not that he was the most traditional guy, but there was a part of him that enjoyed the pursuit of a woman—the hunt, as some would say. The more Khamil thought about it, the more he realized that it was the women who were the boldest who turned him off the most.

But he didn't want to get ahead of himself. He had chased Jessica, and in the end, she had broken his heart. He'd had female friends over the years who told him he was hung up on that fact, that because Jessica had bruised his ego, he didn't want to give his heart to another. And maybe, he finally conceded, they were right.

Khamil twirled a tendril of Monique's silky hair between his fingers. Was that his problem? Had he been a coward all these years, guarding his heart because he didn't want another woman to break it?

He didn't know. All he knew was that for the first time in years, when he thought of Jessica, he didn't feel the bitterness that he used to. Whether or not that was because of the woman who now laid her head on his shoulder, he wasn't sure.

Whatever the case, it could only be a good thing.

"I'm gonna take a shower," Khamil announced the moment after he stepped into the hotel room and placed the luggage on the floor. At the front desk, he'd almost asked Monique if she wanted separate rooms, but decided against it. The memory of last night had been with him all day, and now that they were actually settling down for the evening, he knew without a doubt that he wanted her by his side, sharing his bed. He wanted to spend the night with her again, making love to her as he had less than twenty-four hours ago, and unless she voiced any opposition to spending the night with him, he'd decided there was no reason for him to suggest otherwise.

"All right," Monique said. She lowered herself onto the edge of the king-size bed. "I'm going to make some calls."

Khamil winked at her. "Feel free to join me when you're done."

Monique flashed him a small smile. "Sure."

Leaving Monique sitting on the bed, Khamil sauntered into the bathroom, where he placed his hands on the counter and leaned forward. He stared into the mirror long and hard. He looked like Khamil Jordan. Yet he felt like a different man. Something had changed about him in these last few days, and he wasn't quite sure what it was.

He missed Monique, which didn't make a lick of sense, considering she was just outside the bathroom door. He glanced at the door, hoping it would open, and when it didn't, he felt a modicum of disappointment. When had he ever gone to a hotel room with a woman he wasn't going to make love to? Never.

He wanted her, no doubt about it, and he had to admit that his ego was taking a small beating at the reality that she clearly didn't share his desires. If she wanted him even half as much as he wanted her, she'd be in here with him, ready to get wet . . .

Khamil blew out a ragged breath. Yeah, he had it for her bad. He wanted her in the shower with him, wanted to lather her body up with soap, touch her in all the places that would make her moan . . .

Maybe that was his problem. He was *horny*. A chuckle fell from his lips. How could he not be? The night he'd spent with Monique had been one of the best sexual experiences of his life. She knew just how to move with him, how to touch him. There hadn't been the awkwardness that he usually experienced with a new lover.

Now, he had an erection.

Khamil walked to the bath and turned on the water, adjusting it until it was the right temperature. Maybe he should blast the cold water, he thought with chagrin. What good would it do for him to have an erection when Monique was preoccupied with whatever clue may be at her family's cottage?

And it would certainly be insensitive of him to try

and tempt her away from that to satisfy his carnal urges.

Trying to forget about Monique, Khamil stripped out of his clothes, then got into the bath where he pulled the lever to start the shower. The warm water felt wonderful, sluicing over his body. Closing his eyes, he let the water massage his body and face.

He jumped when he felt a hand brush against him, then whirled around. Opening his eyes, he saw Monique smiling up at him.

A slow grin spread across his face.

"You said I could join you, didn't you?" Monique asked.

"Hell, yeah," Khamil answered. His eyes ventured lower, taking in the view of her exquisite body. No doubt about it, she was perfect. Slim waist, legs for days, full, beautiful breasts, smooth, dark skin. He reached for a nipple, tweaking it with his fingers.

Monique closed her eyes and moaned softly. The nipple puckered at his touch. "You like that?" Khamil asked.

"Mmm."

"How about this?" Lowering his head, he captured the nipple in his mouth.

Monique arched her back and mewed.

"Spread your legs," Khamil told her.

Monique obeyed, and Khamil cupped her, then gently caressed her with his thumb. White-hot heat exploded at the center of her womanhood.

"You like that?"

"Yes," she whimpered.

Khamil dropped to his knees before her, startling Monique. She couldn't tell which was hotter—the water or his breath gently fanning her.

"I want to see you," Khamil said. He ran his

thumb over her nub. "I want to taste you." He flicked his tongue where his thumb had just been.

"Oh, God. . . ." Monique clutched his head and held him to her, luxuriating in the glorious feel of his tongue on her most private spot.

"Damn, Monique. You're driving me crazy."

She couldn't speak, only toss her head from side to side as she moaned. She hardly recognized the passionate cries escaping her, but she'd never felt this good. Khamil flicked his tongue over her, then suckled softly, driving her absolutely mad with desire. With each skillful flick of his tongue, her body coiled tighter and tighter, like a spring.

And then the spring popped, and she dug her nails into his head and cried out as she was catapulted into an abyss of dizzying sensations. Her body rocked with spasms, and still he didn't relent, until Monique was so overcome with the glorious feeling coursing through her body that she collapsed against Khamil. She slithered down and wrapped her arms around his neck.

Khamil kissed her fiercely as the warm water cascaded over their bodies. He wanted to spread her legs and ease himself inside her right then, but the slippery bathtub was hardly ideal. "Let's go to the bed," he whispered.

He stood, helping Monique to her feet as he did. He kissed her once more, then turned off the water. The air in the bathroom instantly chilled them as they got out of the shower, and Khamil quickly reached for a towel. He wrapped it around Monique, rubbing it over her body to help dry her.

Monique stood on her toes and slipped her arms around Khamil's neck. She didn't feel cold when the towel fell from her shoulders into a heap at her feet.

All she could feel was heat as Khamil scooped her into his arms.

And all she could think as he carried her out of the bathroom and set her down on the king-size bed was how much she wanted him, right here and right now, even if it was only for a moment in time.

Sixteen

The next morning, Monique awoke to a feeling of sadness. She wasn't sure why. Her head rested against Khamil's strong chest, and his arms were wrapped snugly around her. She lay listening to the sounds of his steady breathing, as though she'd done this a million times before. There was no denying the comfort level between them, yet something still bothered her.

Monique lifted her head and looked over Khamil's chest to the clock radio. It was only minutes after seven, meaning she hadn't had more than four hours of sleep. She was still tired, but she knew she wouldn't be able to sleep another wink.

Not in Khamil's arms.

Very carefully, Monique slipped out of Khamil's embrace, then sat on the edge of the bed. She threw a glance over her shoulder. Khamil hadn't moved.

What was wrong with her? Both nights she'd spent with Khamil had been wonderful, and during their lovemaking she hadn't been shy about sharing her body with him. But both mornings after had brought a measure of anxiety and distress.

Monique frowned, not quite sure what it was that bothered her. Deciding her energies would be better spent on planning her day, she got up. In her suitcase, she found a T-shirt and slipped it on. Then she walked the few steps to where her purse lay on the sofa. It was early, but her father normally rose with the sun. Before she went to the house, she wanted to let him know about the message she'd received and that she was in Canada to do some investigating.

As Khamil was sleeping, she didn't want to use the room's phone. She dug her cell phone out of her purse and started for the bathroom.

"Monique."

Monique froze, hearing the way Khamil's voice sounded when he called her name. The sweet deepness of his voice, the softness it portrayed as he called her . . . Her stomach suddenly felt like a home for frenzied butterflies.

She turned.

Khamil glanced at the clock, then back at her. "What are you doing?"

"I'm going to make some calls."

"It's eleven minutes after seven," Khamil said matter-of-factly.

"I know that. My father's already up, and I want to—"

"Come back here."

Khamil's statement took Monique by surprise—and made a shiver of desire pass over her.

"Come back here," Khamil repeated.

Khamil's tone left no room for negotiation, and after a moment's hesitation, Monique headed back to the bed.

"Sit down," Khamil told her.

Monique sat. Khamil's eyes roamed over her, from her face to her thighs, then back to her face. He slipped a hand beneath the edge of her T-shirt, resting his fingers on her leg.

"Khamil—" Monique protested.

"Why did you put this on?" Khamil asked, his fingers tugging on the T-shirt.

"Why does anyone put clothes on?" Monique retorted.

"I've already seen all of you," Khamil told her.

"What's your point?"

"Yesterday morning, you got up and left after we made love. Today, you're doing the same thing."

"I've got a lot on my mind."

Khamil edged himself up on an elbow. "It's more than that."

Monique met Khamil's eyes, first wide with indignation, but after a moment, she looked away.

"What are you afraid of, Monique?"

Monique opened her mouth to reply, but nothing came out.

"We've spent two incredible nights together, and you gave me all of you. Yet you can't stay in bed with me the morning after. You don't feel comfortable being naked with me." Khamil slipped a hand beneath the T-shirt and softly stroked one of Monique's breasts.

The delicious feeling that flooded her was too much. She couldn't deal with this, not now. So she stood.

"Monique, don't run away."

Monique swallowed, then met Khamil's eyes. "What's happening between us?"

"We're attracted to each other," Khamil replied simply.

"Yes, but—" Stopping abruptly, Monique turned away.

"But what?"

Monique whirled around. "Is that all it is? Sexual attraction?"

Khamil's shoulders moved in a slight shrug. "Would that be so bad?"

Disappointment swirled in Monique's stomach, making her feel queasy. "I . . . This is the last thing I need."

Khamil sat up fully and reached for her. His hand on her leg, he gently guided her to the bed. "Look, I don't know what's happening between us, either. But I do know . . . Maybe we should go with the flow, see where it takes us."

"I don't need any distractions, Khamil."

Khamil placed a finger on Monique's chin. "Is that all you see me as? A distraction?"

A shaky breath escaped her. "No."

"Good. Because I don't want to be a distraction."

"What do you want with me?" she asked.

"I could think of a number of things," Khamil replied, a devilish grin prancing on his lips as he trailed his fingers from her chin to her ear.

For a moment, Monique was stunned, her throat too constricted for speech. Khamil's sexy smile and suggestive words suddenly had her tingling with longing. For a moment, she felt totally sexy and utterly desirable.

But she said, "I'm serious, Khamil."

Khamil dropped his hand. "I don't know."

His response upset Monique more than she'd expected. She had no clue what she wanted, yet hearing Khamil say that left her feeling . . . empty. She wanted him to care more. She wanted to know she meant more to him than anyone else did.

Her heart thumped quick and hard. God, what was happening to her? But the question was rhetorical, for she knew. Somewhere along the line, she'd started caring for Khamil more than she'd ever planned to.

"I don't want this to mean nothing," Monique whispered, surprised to find she'd voiced her thoughts aloud.

Khamil merely nodded, leaving Monique feeling more insecure than she'd imagined possible. When had she started caring?

Maybe it was because Khamil seemed to understand her, understand her need to resolve the one thing that haunted her most in life. She hadn't found that level of care or understanding from any other man she'd dated. Every other man thought she was obsessed and needed to "let go." Even her family felt the same way.

Yet Khamil hadn't said those words to her. Instead, here he was with her in Toronto to help her get answers.

"Have you ever been in love?" Monique suddenly asked.

A muscle in Khamil's jaw flinched, and his dark eyes grew even darker. But that was the only evidence he had heard her question, because he stared straight ahead, silent.

"Khamil?"

"Yeah." His voice was quiet, and Monique was sure she heard a hint of resentment in his tone.

"What happened?" Monique couldn't help asking. Why this was important to her, she wasn't sure.

"It didn't work out," Khamil replied nonchalantly.

Something flickered in his eyes as he looked at her. Pain. Anger. Khamil had a way with women, a confidence and ease that made Monique believe he'd left a string of broken hearts across the U.S. Yet there was no doubt that Khamil's expression was one of hurt.

Was it possible that someone had broken his playboy heart?

Yes. The pain she saw in his eyes was real.

"She hurt you," Monique said simply.

"Uh-huh. She cheated on me once she realized I no longer had a shot at playing pro ball."

"I'm sorry," Monique said.

"No big deal. That was a long time ago."

It may have been a long time ago, but he was still hurt. Monique could see that as plainly as she could see the sun shining outside the hotel window.

Khamil stretched, and Monique couldn't help but admire his wide shoulders, finely cut arms, and slim torso. Every part of him was so well toned, so taut with muscles. He was a big man, one who Monique knew would never let anything bad happen to her.

Was that part of his appeal?

"We've got to see about getting a car," Khamil announced.

"Oh." Monique sounded disappointed.

"You said your cottage is about an hour away, didn't you?"

"Yes."

"So unless we take a cab, we're going to have to rent a car."

"Mmm-hmm," Monique agreed.

Khamil gave her an odd look. He saw confusion written on her face, which matched the way he felt. Instinctively, he knew that she was disappointed that he had changed the subject from his love life to the reason they were here. But his bad experience with Jessica was something Khamil didn't want to discuss, and as far as he was concerned, it was better left in the past.

Khamil swung his legs off the bed. "So what do you want to do? Call your father?"

"Yeah. I want to tell him what I'm doing."

"You want some privacy?"

"No, I'm cool."

Khamil stood. Catching Monique off guard, he swept her into his arms, pressing her soft body against his hard one. But the kiss he gave her was surprisingly gentle. "Give me a few minutes to get dressed; then I'll head downstairs."

"You don't have to do that, Khamil."

He brushed his lips across her forehead. "It's okay. I brought some work with me."

Khamil released her. Her heart filling with warmth, Monique watched as he dressed. She'd been so wrong with her first impression of him. He had a sensitive, caring side, one she'd never imagined.

And it endeared her to him.

"I'll see you in a bit," Khamil said, then left the hotel room.

When he was gone, Monique sat on the edge of the bed. A sigh oozed out of her. She was afraid of what she was feeling, because her attraction to Khamil had taken her by surprise. No other man had ever made her feel quite the way Khamil was making her feel. But she'd witnessed so many relationships that went bad, including her own parents'.

Her father and mother had fought often, more in the years just before her mother's death. Julia traveled a lot, and from the arguments Monique had overheard, Lucas hadn't approved of all the time she spent away from home. The night her mother had died, her parents had argued. Monique had only overheard loud voices, and wasn't sure what they'd argued about. And she hadn't come out of her room when her father had stormed off. Later, he'd told her and the police that he'd headed back to New York because he and her mother had had a nasty argument, which is why he hadn't been around when she'd been murdered.

The few times Monique had spoken to her father about that night's events, she'd sensed the guilt he carried. If he hadn't argued with her mother and left, she would probably still be alive.

Unfortunately, it was exactly his account of what had happened that night that had led the police to consider him as the prime suspect.

Despite their problems, her father had loved her mother, of that Monique was sure. He couldn't have killed her, much less left her to die in the same house where his daughter slept.

Monique grabbed the receiver and dialed her father's number. After two rings, he answered.

"Hi, Daddy," Monique said, a smile spreading on her face.

"Monique. Hello."

"How are you?"

"I'm okay, sweetheart."

"You sound out of breath."

"I was just heading outside to do some gardening when the phone rang, so I ran to get it." He inhaled a deep breath. "I'm surprised. You're calling early."

"Yeah. I wanted to let you know that I'm in Canada."

"Canada?" Lucas asked, clearly surprised.

Instantly, Monique's back stiffened, bracing for the disapproval she had come to expect from her father where the subject of her mother's murder was concerned. "Dad, I got an anonymous message via my agent. Someone said that I should check the house, that there's some clue to Mom's murder there."

"And you up and ran to Canada as soon as you got this message? What's wrong with you, girl?"

Lucas's words stung Monique, much like a slap in the face. "You know why I came. One of us had to, and it sure as hell wouldn't be you!"

"Don't you take that tone with me."

Years of frustration finally found a voice. "You know what I don't understand, Daddy? Why you haven't done more to find Mom's killer. Fine, you went through hell with the police investigation and being suspected of the crime. But for God's sake, she was your wife. If you loved her, how can you not spend every waking hour trying to find the truth?"

"Sometimes the truth is better left alone."

Monique paused, then asked, "What on earth does that mean?"

"When you search for the truth, you have to be prepared for what you may find. It might not be what you expect, maybe even something you can't live with. Are you prepared for that?"

Monique felt a strange tingling on her nape. "Why are you talking like this? Is there something you know that you're not telling me?"

"Leave it alone, Monique."

"Leave what alone?" she asked, pressing the issue. If her father knew something, why hadn't he told the police?

"Did it occur to you that this could be some kind of trap? That the person who killed your mother wants to get you to the house so they can do you harm?"

Monique's body trembled at her father's words. After a moment, she said, "Yes, Daddy, it did occur to me. But I don't believe that's the case. If someone wanted to hurt me, they'd be taking a big chance in hoping that I'd head to the cottage just because they called and left some cryptic message."

"Unless they know how determined you are to solve this case, and therefore know that you'd be on the first plane out of town."

Her father's statement gave Monique pause. Was that the case? Was someone trying to set her up?

Monique's eyes wandered to the hotel room door. For the first time since she'd arrived in Toronto, she felt genuine fear. And she was glad that Khamil had insisted on coming with her.

Yesterday, she'd thought she knew what she was doing. Now, she was confused. "But, Daddy, if someone is trying to set me up as you suggest, and it's someone who knows we still have the cottage in Barrie, then that means someone close to us killed Mom . . ."

"I want you to head home, Monique. Right now. If the police are reinvestigating the case, fine, let them do their job. I want you to be no part of this."

An eerie feeling passed over Monique, the feeling that her father knew more than he was telling her. Good Lord, what was going on?

"I don't understand, Daddy."

"You heard me." He paused, and when he spoke again, his voice cracked. "I already lost your mother. I don't want to lose you, too."

Monique's throat clogged with emotion. "You won't lose me."

"Please, Monique. Let the police deal with this."

Monique's body was so filled with fear, her hands shook as she held the phone. Part of her conceded that her father was right, that perhaps she was in over her head. But the other part knew she couldn't give up now, not if she indeed was close to learning the truth.

"Promise me, Monique."

Help . . . me. . . .

Her father was asking too much, more than she could give. She wanted to forget the helplessness she'd felt that night as her mother lay dying in her arms. She wanted to forget the image of all that blood that was permanently etched in her brain. She wanted to forget how her mother had begged for help, and that she hadn't been able to help her.

Monique wanted, needed, for the nightmare of what had happened that night to finally end. It wouldn't end until her mother's killer was apprehended—and until then, she had to do all she could to make sure that happened.

"Daddy, I have to go."

"Monique—"

"Bye," Monique said, then quickly hung up. Her hand lingered on the receiver, a million questions spinning in her mind, leaving her dizzy.

For the first time, she wondered if there was something she was missing, something she *should* know about what had happened that night.

Something that would, like a puzzle, fit together—if she could find all the pieces.

Seventeen

"You haven't touched your food."

Khamil's voice actually startled Monique, she was so absorbed in her thoughts.

She looked up at him, then down at her plate. The scrambled eggs and pancakes were no doubt cold by now, making the thought of eating even less appealing than when she had entered this restaurant.

Monique pushed the plate away. "I'm not hungry."

"You have to eat something."

Monique replied with a quick shake of the head.

Watching her, Khamil took a bite of his waffle, then washed it down with coffee. Something was bothering her. He'd known that the moment he'd returned to the room. She'd been tense, preoccupied. He'd asked her what was wrong, but she hadn't answered.

Feeling his gaze, Monique met his eyes. "Are you almost finished?"

Khamil gestured to his side order of bacon in response. "Not yet."

Monique blew out a harried breath. "I'd kinda like to get going."

"We will," Khamil told her.

A frown played on Monique's lips. She balled a

fist, then placed it against her mouth. A second later, she closed her eyes.

Khamil placed his fork and knife against his plate. "Monique, will you please tell me what's wrong?"

Opening her eyes, she looked at him. "I just want to get to the house. That's all."

"You're not going to be any good to yourself if you head up there on an empty stomach. You need energy, Monique. You don't know what you're looking for. We could be there for hours."

"Don't you think I know that?" she quipped. Then her face crumbled. "God, I can't deal with this. . . ."

"Damn it, Monique." Khamil stared at her with concern. "What's going on with you?"

"I need answers. That's what's going on."

"And we're going to get them. Today."

Monique gave a brief nod, but her expression lacked confidence. She said, "I'm starting to wonder if there's more going on than I ever realized."

Khamil's eyebrows shot up. "What do you mean?"

"I mean . . ." Monique fiddled with the stem of her water goblet. "I spoke with my father, and he doesn't want me going to the house. Khamil, he almost sounded as if he knew who killed my mother."

"What?"

Monique shook her head. "I don't know. He didn't say that, so I could be jumping to conclusions. But he said some weird things to me for the first time that have me wondering how much he knows."

"I don't understand, Monique."

"Neither do I."

Khamil watched her, watched her rest her cheek in her palm and glance away. He could almost see the burden on her shoulders.

"I know this is hard, Monique," he began gently.

"But trust me, you have to take care of yourself. Not eating won't help the situation."

Monique wanted to eat, but her stomach was a ball of nerves, and she knew she wouldn't be able to keep anything down if she tried.

"I . . ." She glanced down at her plate and instantly felt queasy. "I can't."

Khamil swallowed a piece of bacon, then spoke. "What about the Canadian police? Are you going to contact them before you head to the house?"

"I thought about calling that detective who's in charge of my mother's cold case, but . . ."

"But what?"

Monique shrugged. "I'll call after I check the house and see if there's any type of clue there." And she suddenly wasn't sure of anything anymore, least of all if she should call the police. "I don't know."

"What?"

"It's just . . ." Monique's voice trailed off. "My father was the prime suspect for a long time, but ultimately, the police didn't have enough evidence to charge him. He always maintained that he had nothing to do with the murder, and all these years, I believed him. But—" Monique stared into Khamil's eyes. "But, Khamil, what if I'm wrong?"

Nearly two hours later, Khamil pulled their rented Jeep Cherokee up in front of a quaint-looking cabin on a small street in Barrie. The cabin was surrounded by brush, and the grass clearly hadn't been cut in years. Wildflowers and weeds grew all around, making the cabin seem as if it were part of a wilderness landscape.

The nearest house was approximately twenty feet away on either side.

Khamil turned and found Monique staring ahead blankly.

"Hey," he said.

"It's been so long," Monique whispered. Her father had never sold the house, partly because she'd insisted that he not do so. But she hadn't been back here since her mother's death.

Once, this place had held so many happy memories for Monique and her family. She and her mother had come here to spend many summers, her father joining them when he had his two weeks of summer vacation. The times they'd been here, her parents had rarely argued. Except for that fateful night . . .

"You sure you want to do this?" Khamil asked.

Monique looked at him and nodded. "Yes. I have to."

"All right." Khamil opened his car door, got out, then went to the passenger side and opened the door for Monique. When she didn't make a move, he extended his hand.

Monique took his hand, thankful to have him with her, thankful for the strength he was offering. She climbed out of the Jeep.

"You have the key?" Khamil asked.

A small smile touched Monique's lips. "Yes," she replied. "Wouldn't that be something for me to get all the way here, only to have forgotten the key?"

"We would have gotten in somehow."

Monique met Khamil's eyes. "I'm sure we would have."

"It's nice to see you smile," Khamil told her. "You have such a beautiful smile."

"Thank you." The smile wavered, and Monique bit down hard on her bottom lip. "God, Khamil. I'm so afraid."

"Hey." Draping an arm around Monique's shoulder, Khamil drew her to him. He could only empathize with what she was going through, but he knew this had to be incredibly hard. He still had trouble going into his little nephew's room when he visited Javar and Whitney in Chicago.

Monique blew out a loud breath. "Okay. Let's do this."

Taking her hand, Khamil walked with Monique to the porch. There, she dug the key out of her purse and slipped it into the lock. A second later, she pushed the door open.

The smell of dust and mold was the first thing that hit Monique; then sadness hit her in the gut. The last time she'd been here, she and her mother had giggled happily as they'd stepped over the threshold.

Help . . . me. . . .

Monique shook her head, trying to lose the memory.

"It's not too late to change your mind," Khamil said.

"No." Monique swallowed and squared her shoulders. "I have to do this."

She stepped away from Khamil, walking farther into the house. "She's been gone for years, but I feel her." Monique did a three-hundred-and-sixty-degree turn. "I feel her everywhere."

"Where did it happen?"

Monique faced Khamil, then pointed to the door beside her. "In this room."

The next second, she reached for the door's handle. The door creaked in protest as she slowly opened it.

Help . . . me. . . .

Monique's knees buckled. But before she fell, Khamil's strong arms were around her.

As Khamil held Monique, her breathing came in

quick, ragged gasps. He glanced into the room. It was completely empty, as though it had never been lived in, but he felt a presence there.

"My father got rid of everything in this room, but I can still see it. I don't even have to close my eyes."

Khamil placed a hand on Monique's, taking it off the door's handle. Then he closed the door. "If there's nothing in this room, then there's nothing here that can help us."

Monique's gaze flitted to Khamil's. "Yes, you're right. You're right."

With the door closed, Monique stood tall once again. Khamil ran both hands down the length of her arms. "All right. The caller said something about letters."

"Yes."

"Where might they be?"

Monique's eyes went to the staircase. "There's a loft up there, where we kept a lot of things. From what I remember, my mother had a chest of personal items up there. Memorabilia from her career and whatnot."

"Then that's where we go."

Khamil led the way. The stairs squeaked as they made their way up.

In the loft, dust mites flew in the air. The area was large and housed several items, all of which were covered by large, white sheets.

Monique sauntered to the large bay window, which let in lots of sunshine. "My cousins and I used to love to hang out up here. We used to spy on all the neighbors. See?" Monique gestured to the house across the street. "You can see right into the backyard from this angle. There were a girl and her brother who used to live there. Talk about spoiled."

"Your cousins used to come here with you?"

Monique faced Khamil. "Uh-huh. See the house on our left? They owned that one."

"Really?"

"Yeah. My mother bought it for them. She liked the idea that we could take family vacations with our extended family. She was very close to my uncle Richard and aunt Sophie."

"Sophie was her sister?"

"No. Uncle Richard is my father's brother. He and Aunt Sophie are divorced now." Monique walked away from the window and to the middle of the room. She grabbed a white blanket and pulled, then waved her hand around as dust flew into the air.

"If my mother had any letters, they should be in her chest," Monique explained. She pulled another blanket off more hidden objects. "Ah. There it is."

She lowered herself to the floor, sitting cross-legged. Khamil sat beside her.

As Monique lifted the lid on the chest, Khamil said, "Tell me about your father."

She looked at him. "My father?"

"Yeah. What does he do?"

"Well, he's retired now, but he used to work as a customs officer at Laguardia. In fact—" Monique smiled. "That's how he met my mother."

"You're kidding."

"Nope. She was heading back to New York from France, I believe, and she went through the line my father was manning. He fell for her instantly, asked for her number, and the rest is history."

"Wow. It's like they were destined to meet."

"Yeah." Monique's voice became wistful. "This was the one place I remember them being happy."

"They had a rough marriage?"

Monique shrugged nonchalantly. "No worse than anyone else's, I don't think. Uncle Richard and Aunt

Sophie always argued. My dad once told me that the Savard men were very passionate in every way. They didn't hide their emotions. My mother traveled a lot, and my dad missed her. I think that was their biggest problem. I think that was my aunt and uncle's biggest problem, too. Uncle Richard is a pilot, and he was always away from home. And I'm not sure if this is true, but Aunt Sophie always thought Uncle Richard was having affairs."

"That's rough."

"From what my cousin, Doreen, used to tell me, Aunt Sophie was pretty paranoid about the whole issue."

"Distrust like that is enough to drive two people apart."

"I know."

"And your parents?"

"Infidelity was not an issue," Monique quickly said. "My dad was thirteen years older than my mother. He didn't get married until he was forty. He told me he'd waited all his life to meet the right woman, and when he met my mother, he knew she was the one. He was devoted to her. Which is why he missed her so much when she was away for work. Then, when she started getting weird letters from fans . . ." Monique's eyes lit up. "Maybe that's what that caller was referring to. A letter from the guy who was obsessed with my mother."

Monique quickly began going through the items in the box. She pulled out two large scrapbooks, then placed them on the floor.

"May I take a look at this?" Khamil asked.

"Sure."

Monique continued rummaging through the contents of the chest while Khamil opened one of the scrapbooks. Aside from the scrapbooks, there were family photo albums, some framed photos, and a large quilt.

"Wow. Your mother was beautiful," Khamil commented.

Pausing, Monique looked at him. "Yeah, she was. She was still modeling at forty-two, when she died."

"Really?"

"Yep. Her skin was flawless and smooth, even at that age. She didn't look a day over twenty-five."

"I see why she was a successful model." Khamil flipped a page. "Elise Skin Care?"

"Uh-huh. That was her biggest contract."

Khamil turned the page. A grin spread on his face. "Hey, is that you?"

Monique leaned forward, and Khamil held the scrapbook toward her. She giggled as she looked at the picture of her and her mother, both wearing white sundresses, Monique sitting beside her mother, resting her head against her shoulder. "Yeah, that's me."

"You two modeled together?"

"Yeah. My mother negotiated a contract for me with Elise Skin Care as well, so we could work together. Because she was spending more and more time away from home, she wanted to be with me as much as she could. That was my first experience modeling. They loved the idea of having mother and daughter model together. I guess they were trying to say that if you used their products, you could look as young as my mother did. Of course, my mother naturally looked like that, with no help from Elise."

Khamil chuckled. "She didn't use their products?"

Flashing him a wry grin, Monique shook her head.

Khamil turned to another page, and Monique went back to the chest. She lifted the heavy quilt and placed it on the floor.

Then her breath caught in her throat.

There were envelopes—several of them—lining the bottom of the chest.

"Khamil," she said. When he looked at her, she announced, "I found the letters."

Eighteen

"How many are there?" Khamil asked.

Monique reached for a stack of letters secured with an elastic band, pulling it out of the chest. "A lot."

Khamil extended a hand. "Here. Give me some."

Monique passed him the stack.

"What am I looking for?" Khamil asked.

"I don't know," Monique replied, pulling out another stack of letters. *"Anything."*

She slipped the elastic band off the letters she held, then lifted the first letter in the pile. "This is my father's handwriting," she said. She flipped through the envelopes. "These all are from him."

"He wrote her a lot of letters?"

"I guess so. She was away a lot."

Monique reached inside the chest and took out more letters. She didn't want to read the letters her father had written to her mother. Not only did it seem like an invasion of their privacy, there was no point in reading her father's letters, as she was sure they didn't hold the clue the caller had been talking about.

Monique sifted through the news envelopes. The penmanship on all were different, leading her to believe these were from her mother's fans. "There might be something here," she said. "I think this is fan mail."

"This letter is from your father to your mother," Khamil announced. "I don't know if you want me reading it."

Monique smiled, appreciating his concern. "Go ahead." She paused. "I think you're the better person to read those, anyway—just in case I've been blinded by love and family loyalty all these years."

Khamil gave her an understanding nod, then began reading the letter.

For the next several minutes, Monique and Khamil read letter after letter. Finally, Monique said, "I don't think there's anything in these. They're all nice fan letters, telling my mother that they admire her, that they like the skin care products—stuff like that." Monique groaned. "I'm not even sure the mail from her stalker would be in here. The police probably have it."

"So far, these are all love letters from your father to your mother. You're right. He adored her."

"Yeah," Monique agreed absently. She withdrew another bunch of envelopes. This was like searching for a needle in a haystack, only she didn't know what the needle looked like!

She opened another envelope and scanned the letter. She was about to toss it aside until she saw the words *I'll always love you.*

Her interest piqued, Monique's eyes went back to the first line. She began reading.

Dear Julia,

I miss you, more than you could ever imagine. It's lonely here without you. I hate when we have to say goodbye, and miss you the first second we're apart. I hate having to keep my feelings for you secret. I know this is a tough situation, but there must be a way we can work it out. I can't imagine not being able to be with you forever, freely. We've both tried to protect everyone else, putting our own feelings aside. I can't do that any longer. I need to be with you, Julia. Now and forever.

I'll always love you.

Your Pooh-Bear

"Monique."

At the sound of Khamil's voice, Monique looked at him.

"My God, Monique. What's wrong?"

A sick feeling was swirling inside her body. God, what did this letter mean? It wasn't from her father.

Khamil reached for the letter, taking it from her fingers. After he read it, he asked, "Who's Pooh-Bear?"

"I have no clue."

"It's not your father." It was a statement, not a question.

"Obviously not."

Khamil held Monique's gaze. He saw the pain in her eyes, and didn't know what to say to make this easier for her. "Monique," he began cautiously. "Did you know that your mother was having an affair?"

"No!" She buried her face in her hands, then looked at Khamil once more. "Oh, my God."

Khamil didn't say anything, merely stared at her.

"I know what you're thinking," she suddenly said.

"You do?"

"My father didn't kill my mother. This doesn't prove anything."

"It's motive, Monique."

Monique shot to her feet. "I don't care what you think it is. My father didn't do this."

Khamil stood to meet Monique. "How do you know?"

Monique's lips trembled before answering. "He couldn't have."

Khamil reached for Monique's face, but she stepped away from his touch. After a moment, he said, "Why don't you take a break? I'll go through the rest of the letters."

"No." Monique shook her head. She was missing something, she was sure. There was a memory in her reach, but she couldn't quite grasp it. "I'll keep reading."

Monique dropped to the floor once again and continued going through the letters. Khamil sat beside her, looking over her shoulder as she read. After the fourth letter, Monique knocked the stack across the floor. "Gawd!"

"Monique."

Her eyes flew to Khamil's. "Do *not* tell me this is okay, because it's *not.* God, I've just found out that my mother was having an affair. I can't believe this."

Khamil took both Monique's hands in his. "You know what? I think you should call the police." When Monique whimpered, he continued. "They should know this, Monique." Khamil placed a hand beneath Monique's chin, forcing her to look at him. Her eyes glistened with tears.

"Look, I understand your fear," he said. "The last thing I wanted to believe was that my mother could possibly be responsible for taking my nephew's life, or trying to kill my sister-in-law. But you know what? When we all learned the truth, as painful as it was, it was a relief. The truth won't always make you happy, but it will bring a measure of closure."

"My father asked me if I was prepared to learn

the truth. He said sometimes it's best left alone. Do you think he knew about my mother's affair?"

Khamil palmed her face. "I think he did. Something he said in one of his letters now makes sense."

Monique looked at Khamil expectantly. "What?"

"He said something about forgiving her for what had happened, that he still loved her more than life. That's all."

Monique glanced at the floor, deep in thought. Nothing in life was easy, Khamil realized, knowing how much pain she was going through. Everyone had some issue or other that they were dealing with. But he was a firm believer in the adage that what didn't kill you made you stronger.

And Monique was strong. A survivor. She'd dealt with more than any young child should ever have to deal with, yet she still had a zest for life, a passion she wanted to share. He'd felt that both times they'd made love.

"I think you're right," Monique announced minutes later. "I should call the police." Getting onto her knees, she crawled the few feet to where her purse was. She took out her cell phone and her wallet. She'd placed the number for Detective McKinney in there.

Monique dialed the number for the detective, then waited. When his voice mail came on, she frowned.

"What?" Khamil asked.

"I got his voice mail," she explained. "It's the weekend." Looking down at her paper, she began punching in another number.

"Who are you calling now?"

"He left me his home number as well."

As Monique listened to the phone ring, Khamil watched her. She chewed on her bottom lip and thrummed her fingers against her thigh.

Her eyes lit up. "Hello. I'm looking for Detective McKinney." She threw a relieved glance Khamil's way, and anxiety danced in his stomach. "Hello, Detective McKinney. This is Monique Savard. I'm sorry to call you at home. . . ."

Khamil rose to his feet and sauntered to the window, affording Monique some privacy as she spoke to the detective. He glanced outside. The branches of the large maple tree outside the window swayed in the gentle breeze. As his eyes roamed through the tree, he spotted a nest filled with eggs.

Just then, a sparrow flew by the window, landing on the branch with the nest. The bird was so close that if the glass weren't in the way, Khamil could reach out and touch it.

It was a sight he didn't see in New York City, and it filled his heart with warmth.

Yeah, this place was idyllic. Here, surrounded by nature, one had to sit back, relax, and enjoy.

He glanced over his shoulder at Monique. A lump formed in his throat as he looked at her hunched form. He wished they could be here under different circumstances—on a romantic getaway, rather than a search for her mother's killer.

Maybe. One day.

Khamil turned back to the window. The sparrow was now nestled on her eggs. Children needed their mothers, no matter how old they got. Monique's mother's life had been cut short. His mother had been taken from him due to her own crazy actions.

They had something in common. Maybe that's why he felt such a strong pull toward her. That and the fact that he sensed her vulnerability, and Khamil wasn't one to walk away from someone who needed him.

"Khamil."

Khamil turned when he heard his name. "You told him?"

Monique got to her feet. "I told him, but he already knew."

Khamil frowned. "He did?"

Monique strolled toward him, then passed him and went to the window. She leaned a hip against the frame. After a moment of staring outside, she faced Khamil. "I'm not sure what's real anymore."

Khamil walked over to her. "What do you mean?"

"There's so much my father didn't tell me. I'm not sure if he thought I was too young to know, or . . ." Monique whimpered.

"You don't want to tell me?" Khamil asked gently.

Monique met his eyes. "Of course I'll tell you. You're the only one who seems to care." Monique paused, then continued. "Detective McKinney knew that my mother had had an affair. Apparently, another man's sperm was found in her body when they did the autopsy. When they questioned my father about it, he told the cops that he knew my mother was seeing someone else."

"Wait a second. Are you saying that on the night of your mother's murder, she'd been with someone else?"

Monique squeezed her head with both hands. "I remember my parents fighting. I remember my father leaving. But I had no clue anyone came over after he left. Other than the person who killed her."

"Maybe . . ." Khamil paused. "Do you think your mother may have been raped?"

"I asked the detective that. But he said that there was no sign of force at all. And . . ." Monique blew out a quick breath. "My mother was also pregnant."

"What?"

Monique shook her head, still unable to believe

all she'd learned. "If it was my father's child, wouldn't my parents have told me about the baby?" She hugged her torso, suddenly cold. "God, maybe that's why my parents were arguing that night."

"Hey." Khamil's eyes lit up. "If someone else had been with your mother after your father left, then doesn't that exonerate your father?"

Warmth flooded Monique's body as she stared at Khamil. Ever since her mother's murder, she had wanted her family members to say something as simple as this, but they never had. She knew they were secretly convinced of her father's guilt. That Khamil offered her a reason to once again believe in her father, given the new evidence, meant the world to her.

Lord help her, she was falling for him.

Hard.

"I was so wrong about you."

"Excuse me?"

Khamil's question made Monique realize that she'd spoken aloud. A smile played on her lips as she met Khamil's eyes. "I said, I was wrong about you."

"Oh?"

"You don't want to know what I thought about you in the beginning." She chuckled softly.

"If the way you rebuffed me is any indication, I can only imagine." But he smiled, letting her know whatever she may have felt before didn't bother him now.

"I thought you were—" She grinned sheepishly. "Well, I thought you figured the world revolved around you."

Khamil flashed her a surprised look. "It doesn't?"

Monique laughed. "You're so silly."

"I'm just glad I can make you smile." Khamil softly stroked her cheek.

Monique's laugh faded. "Yeah. So am I." Once

again, her expression grew serious. "I want to believe my father had nothing to do with my mother's death, but the detective raised a good point. What if my father came back to the house, saw my mother's lover leaving, and became enraged? My father was never able to verify his whereabouts after he left this house that night. He said he drove to Toronto and went to the airport, but wasn't able to catch a flight back to New York until the morning. I never wanted to consider this, but that would have given him enough time to head back up here . . ." Monique stopped abruptly, unable to go on.

Instantly, Khamil swept her into his arms. Monique sagged against his strong chest, feeling as though his strength was helping her to carry this heavy burden.

"Until we know otherwise," Khamil said, "don't think the worst. I know you, Monique. I can understand your loyalty to your father, but I don't think it's unfounded. You're smart. I know you'd rather know the truth, no matter how horrible, than stick your head in the sand."

A soft moan escaped her, and Monique was surprised to feel a tear run down her cheek. How did Khamil know her so well in such a short time? He was absolutely right. She hadn't pursued the truth for this long without knowing that she had to be prepared for the worst, no matter how inconceivable it might be.

I love you, she thought.

Monique pulled her head back and looked up at Khamil. He looked down at her. She felt a little jolt in her chest.

God, it was true. She'd gone and fallen in love with him.

As Khamil stared down at her, the edges of his mouth curled in the slightest of smiles. His eyes were full of compassion, and something else she couldn't quite read.

Did he feel about her the same way she felt about him?

The thought caused her stomach to churn with anxiety.

He was here for her, being a wonderful friend to her, giving her the support that she so desperately needed. But maybe this was simply about friendship—nothing more.

Before she knew what was happening, Khamil covered her mouth with his. A surprised squeal bubbled out of her throat, but Khamil caught it with his tongue.

Monique instantly melted in his arms, her head growing light with desire. Never before had a man's kiss made her dizzy the way Khamil's did.

She could get used to this.

Monique's cell phone rang. Startled, both Khamil and Monique jumped apart. Then they laughed.

Khamil rested his forehead against hers. "You better get that."

"Yeah."

The phone continued to ring. Groaning, Khamil stepped away from her. Monique ran to retrieve her phone.

"Hello?"

"Monique, it's Doreen."

"Hey. What's up?"

"You tell me."

Monique glanced at Khamil. He mouthed, "Who is it?"

She mouthed back, "My cousin." Into the phone, she said, "I guess you heard."

"You're in *Canada*?"

"Yes. My father called you?"

"He got off the phone with my mother a couple hours ago. I've been trying to reach you, but kept getting your message service."

"I didn't turn my phone on until recently," Monique explained.

"Your father's really worried about you, and frankly, so am I. He said you got a call about some clue at the house."

"Yes." Briefly, Monique filled her cousin in on the call that had come to her agent, then what she'd learned about her mother's infidelity.

"Holy," Doreen said.

"I think my father was trying to protect me," Monique explained.

"Or keep the truth from you for other reasons."

Monique hesitated, then said, "Yeah. Maybe."

"Hon, I know you've always thought I don't understand, but I do. You've gone through so much pain already. What if you learn something you'd be better off not knowing?"

"Like the fact that my father may have killed my mother?"

"Yeah."

"Nothing can be worse than the fact that I held my mother in my arms as she died. I want to know the truth, Doreen, no matter what."

"I hope so." Doreen spoke as if it were already common knowledge that Lucas Savard was guilty of the crime. "I'm talking to Monique. Wait a sec—"

Monique heard some rumbling, then, "Monique."

That was Daniel's voice, stern.

"Daniel, hi."

"So, you're up at the cottage."

"Yeah." She didn't want to hear her cousin's disapproval. "I already told Doreen everything. She can fill you in."

"So, someone called you?"

"Someone called my agent, yes."

"Who?"

"I don't know."

"What did they say?"

Monique sighed. "Like I already told Doreen, the person said something about there being letters at the cottage, that these letters would give me answers."

"And?" Daniel prompted.

"I did find some letters. Letters that make it clear my mother was having an affair."

"That doesn't surprise me."

"*Excuse* me?"

"Look, Monique," Daniel went on, ignoring her. "Everyone's worried about you. Why don't you give up this wild-goose chase and just come home? How do you know that whoever called you isn't setting you up?"

"I'm fine," Monique told him.

"You're just so stubborn, Monique. First, *America's Most Wanted,* now this. You may as well put a target on your head and stand in the middle of Times Square."

Monique rolled her eyes. "I'm fine," she reiterated. She looked to Khamil. "I'm here with someone."

"You are?" Daniel was clearly shocked.

"I'm smarter than you all give me credit for. Now, why did you say that it doesn't surprise you that my mother had an affair?"

"Who's with you?" Daniel asked.

"A friend," Monique replied testily. "Look, Daniel, if there's something you know that I don't—"

"Seems to me you have all the answers you were looking for."

"I only know that my mother was having an affair." She was getting annoyed. "I don't know who killed her."

There was a pause, then Daniel said, "Did it ever occur to you that someone was trying to protect you—spare you from the truth?"

Was there a conspiracy going on in her family? Did everyone else know something except she? And if so, what? "I'm a big girl now," she said.

"Come home, Monique."

"Tell me what you know."

"Get on the first plane and get out of there. Leave the past in the past, Monique."

"Do you know who killed my mother?" she asked.

"You heard me," Daniel snapped.

There was dead air. "Daniel? Daniel." Monique grunted as her eyes went to Khamil. "He hung up on me."

"That didn't go well, I take it."

Monique shook her head.

"Who's Daniel?"

"He's my other cousin. He and Doreen are my uncle Richard and aunt Sophie's children. They used to spend as much time here during the summers as my family did."

"From your end of the conversation, it sounded like Daniel was upset."

Monique folded her arms over her chest. "Daniel's always a little . . . testy. He's manic-depressive, and he has awful mood swings. When he's happy, he's wonderful. But when he's upset, you're best off staying clear from him." Monique ran a hand through her hair. "Plus, Daniel's always been overprotective. You should have seen what he was like when people picked on me or Doreen. I think his overprotective nature developed when he learned, at a young age, that his parents wouldn't live forever. About a year

before my mother died, Aunt Sophie got pretty ill.
For quite some time, she was bedridden with some
mysterious illness the doctors could never quite pin-
point. Because Uncle Richard was away a lot—he
needed to work to support the family—Daniel became the one who took care of his mother. He was
the oldest of the children, but even for a seventeen-
year-old, that was a serious burden. Anyway, I know
for a while he was really scared that he would lose
his mother. So was Doreen. We all were." Monique
paused. "I know he's only upset now because he's
worried about me."

Khamil nodded in understanding. "You think he
knows something and isn't saying?"

"I don't know. He wasn't at all surprised about my
mother's affair. But then, he was four years older than
me. Maybe he was privy to some things that my parents
kept from me, simply because I was younger."

Several moments passed, then Khamil asked,
"What do you want to do?"

"I think I've learned all I'm going to learn here,"
Monique replied, looking around the large loft. As
well, she wasn't sure she could spend much more
time here and not completely break down with the
memory of what had happened sixteen years ago.
The happy memories of the time she'd spent here
were overshadowed by that awful night.

"Besides, it certainly seems like my family knows
more than I do. So"—she met Khamil's eyes—"I
want to go back to New York. I want to find out
exactly what it is that my family has been keeping
from me all these years."

Nineteen

"I'll call you later," Monique told Khamil as she got out of the taxi and stepped onto the sidewalk in front of her building.

"Are you sure you'll be okay?"

"Yes, I'll be fine." Khamil had offered to come up with her, but she had declined. It had been a long day, and Monique's brain was still churning with all she'd learned. Tonight, she simply wanted to take a long, hot bath, then get some much-needed sleep before talking to her family tomorrow.

She continued, "If Raymond was the one who trashed my apartment, he won't be stupid enough to come back here. He'll have to know I called the police."

Khamil didn't respond. Instead, he turned to the driver and passed him some money. A moment later, he stepped out of the taxi.

Monique gawked at him.

"I'm going upstairs with you."

"Khamil." Monique spoke his name in protest. "That's not necessary."

"Humor me," Khamil said. "I want to make sure you're safe. Then I'll leave."

Monique's heart beat faster. The thought of Khamil coming up to her apartment made her think of the two incredible nights they'd shared. And it made her wonder what the future held.

"Okay," she agreed. By now, she knew Khamil well enough to know that he wouldn't take no for an answer.

Minutes later, they were at her apartment door. The locksmith had installed a new lock before she'd left for Toronto, and finding the new key, Monique inserted it.

She paused, throwing a glance over her shoulder at Khamil. He nodded, and Monique opened the door.

Khamil stepped past her into the apartment, and wary, Monique watched him. But after a moment, his shoulders drooped with relief. He faced her. "Seems like the coast is clear."

Monique crossed the threshold into the apartment. "Thanks."

"All right," Khamil said. "I'll go now. Make sure you bolt your door."

"I will."

Khamil slowly strolled out of the apartment, then faced Monique. "Look, if you need anything, anything at all, call me."

Monique offered him a soft smile. "Will do."

Khamil didn't move, instead lingering outside her door, staring at her. Monique's flesh tingled beneath his gaze.

Oh, yes. There was definitely a sexual chemistry between them, and they were wonderful in bed together. But she wanted more than that. Yet what she'd learned about her parents' marriage today made her wonder if a happy relationship was only an illusion.

She asked, "Why are you so good to me?"

"We're friends, right?"

A lump of disappointment soared to Monique's throat from her heart. Forcing a smile, she nodded, unable to say anything.

Khamil raised an eyebrow. "And of course, I love your body."

"Of course." Her voice was clipped, but she couldn't help it. She was disappointed.

The playful expression on Khamil's face disappeared. "What's wrong?"

"Nothing. I'll see you later . . . *friend.*"

Khamil's eyebrows shot together. "What . . ."

"Nothing. Don't mind me. I'm tired."

"Hey," Khamil said softly. "Don't jump to any conclusions. You're a . . ." he paused. "Special friend."

"Sure." Again, she smiled. "Look, thanks for going to Toronto with me. I'll call you tomorrow."

"Okay." Khamil gave her an odd look.

"Good night." Before Khamil could say anything else, Monique closed the door and turned the lock. Disappointment washing over her, she rested her head against the door.

What was wrong with her? Hadn't she known that it was dangerous to care? Her parents hadn't had a good relationship, no matter how much she'd lied and told herself otherwise. Her uncle and aunt hadn't had a good relationship. Daniel's relationship with his girlfriend was constantly up and down.

Why, oh why, did Monique expect a proclamation of undying love from Khamil, a man she'd known was a player the moment she'd seen him?

Still hoping, Monique pressed an ear to the door, listening for sound. Seconds later, she heard the *ping* of the elevator door as it opened.

She closed her eyes tightly, willing the unexpected hurt to pass.

It didn't.

"We're friends," she heard Khamil say.

No doubt, he'd bedded lots of his *friends*.

"Don't do this," Monique told herself. When she'd slept with Khamil, there had been no promises. Indeed, she hadn't wanted any. They'd both been mature adults, sharing the act of sex. It was her fault if she'd read any more into it.

She'd done a helluva lot more than that. She'd gone and fallen in love with him.

Monique wasn't exactly sure when it had happened. But she did know that she loved him. He was in her heart.

Vicky often said that men came and went in your life, that relationships didn't last forever, but that you should take the positive from them, no matter how short they were. Was that what Monique was supposed to do—take the positive out of her experience with Khamil?

Exhaling a sigh, Monique walked down the hallway to the bathroom. She needed to take that hot bath. Trying to forget Khamil and her feelings for him, she sat on the edge of her Jacuzzi tub and started the bathwater, then added a liberal amount of lavender scented bubble bath. As it ran, she headed to the bedroom, where she checked her messages.

"Hey, girl," came Vicky's voice. "Give me a call. I think we need to straighten some things out."

Monique couldn't help it; she felt a spurt of anger. She wasn't sure she wanted to call Vicky back. For years, they'd been friends, and she never would have let a man come between them. Clearly, Vicky didn't share the same sentiment.

Beep. "Monique." Pause. "It's Raymond. Look, I need to talk to you. Call me. Please."

Beep. "Hey, Monique. It's me again. You need to

call me. I got a weird message, and I think it pertains to you and the search for your mother's killer."

Beep. "Monique, it's Raymond. I hope you're not avoiding me. We need to talk. I'm sorry if I acted like a jerk, but there are some things I need to tell you, things you need to know."

"Whatever," Monique said. The last thing she'd do was call Raymond back. After what the man had done to her apartment, she wanted nothing to do with the psycho.

Having heard all the messages, Monique went back to the bathroom. The tub was almost full and she turned off the faucets. Next, she stripped out of her jeans and T-shirt, then slowly eased herself into the warm water.

"Mmm," she said aloud. The water felt good.

She laid her head back and closed her eyes, staying like that for several minutes. When was the last time she'd relaxed like this? Too long ago for her to even remember. It was something she needed to do more often. Already, the warm water was working out the kinks in her neck.

Monique reached for her sponge and dipped it in the water, then held it above her body and squeezed, releasing a waterfall of bubbles and steam. Her mind drifted back to Khamil. She knew she needed to forget him, but how could she? Already, she regretted sending him home instead of asking him to spend the night with her.

She missed him, missed his warm embrace. She missed what they'd shared just last night in the shower at the hotel.

A quivering sensation ran throughout her body as she remembered the feel of Khamil's lips on her body. Never had a man's tongue felt so good before,

so much so that she craved it now, craved it as a
nicotine addict craved a cigarette.

She closed her eyes and let herself imagine . . .

Khamil was resting against the doorjamb of the
bathroom, his lips curved in the slightest of grins. His
eyes were dark with desire as they probed every inch
of Monique's wet body. Slowly, he entered the bathroom, pulled his T-shirt over his head, and slipped out
of his perfectly snug jeans. His body was magnificent,
corded with muscles in all the right places.

And he was ready for her. His erection was testa-
ment to that.

How she wanted him! She needed him in this tub
with her, his slick body pressed against hers.

"Khamil."

A seductive smile spread on his face as he approached her. Stepping into the steaming bathtub,
Khamil gradually lowered himself on top of Monique's moistened body. She closed her eyes and un-
leashed a soft, passionate moan.

With exquisite tenderness, Khamil explored every
part of her body with his hands. Caressing. Tweaking.
Fondling. Teasing. Mercilessly, he ran his tongue along
her wet, hot skin, tormenting her with passion as he
glided his tongue in circles around one of her taut,
throbbing peaks. And just when Monique thought she
was going to go crazy with desire, Khamil took her
nipple in his mouth and sucked, sending ripples of
pleasure coursing through her. Monique arched her
back in heated longing.

"Oh, Khamil." Her own voice startled her, and the
cold realization hit her.

Khamil was nowhere near the bathroom.

Lord, she had it for the man bad!

Never, ever, had Monique gotten so absorbed in a
sexual fantasy the way she had just now. Her body

was thrumming with sexual longing, for which there was no cure.

Except Khamil.

But while his body would satisfy her physical needs, she needed more than that. She wanted all of him—body and soul.

Groaning, Khamil turned from his back onto his side. He adjusted his head against the pillow, then promptly rolled onto his stomach.

He closed his eyes, but a moment later, they popped open. Oh, what was the use? He'd been tossing and turning since he'd gotten into bed more than an hour and a half ago. He could no more sleep than he could stop thinking about Monique.

"Monique." Her name escaped his lips on a sigh.

He felt a niggling of disappointment. He didn't like how things had ended between them earlier. He had known what she wanted from him, yet he hadn't been able to give it to her.

He'd recognized that spark in her eyes, the same spark that he'd seen in the eyes of so many of the other women he'd dated. No matter how much she had fussed and rebuffed him in the beginning, she'd fallen for him.

And that scared the crap out of Khamil.

Monique was beautiful, caring. Strong, yet vulnerable. The sexual chemistry between them was undeniable. He hadn't felt such a strong attraction for a woman since . . .

Since Jessica.

And that was the problem, he realized. He'd fallen hard for Jessica, given her his heart completely. And she'd hurt him.

The reality that after all these years, he was finally

feeling another strong attraction for a woman had him in a quandary. Over the years, he'd learned to turn off his emotions, to guard his heart. Yet there was something about Monique that had made him let that guard down.

But he didn't want the guard down. He wanted it back up around his heart.

Rolling onto his back, Khamil blew out a frustrated breath. Man, he really *was* afraid of getting hurt. He had never quite acknowledged his feelings over the years since Jessica had broken his heart, no matter what his friends had told him. Instead, he'd concentrated on having fun. And he'd turned into the heartbreaker, all so that he wouldn't get too close to anyone.

Wow. The realization shocked him.

He was thirty-eight years old. Certainly he couldn't go on like this forever. Yet the thought of taking a chance on a relationship with Monique scared him more than he cared to admit.

Khamil turned onto his side, lay there for a moment, then promptly sat up. He flicked on the light on his end table. With the room illuminated, he stood and walked across the bedroom to his closet. Reaching inside, he found his guitar and took it out.

Khamil went back to the bed, where he sat, positioning the guitar in his arms, ready to play. It had been ages since he'd touched it.

He strummed a few chords, getting used to the feel and sound of it. And then he was playing the tune to DeBarge's "A Dream," thinking of Monique.

Thinking of her and how she fit the lyrics.

He wanted to turn the fantasy he dreamed of— that he had finally found the woman to spend his life with—into reality.

For years, the dream had eluded him. What he'd

experienced with Monique in the last few days had made the dream come alive again. Unlike DeBarge, he didn't want to wake up knowing that the dream would never come true.

But dreams didn't come true without any effort.

He'd put forth that effort in his career for years and had achieved success. He'd never let fear of failure stop him. Why let fear of rejection get the best of him now?

It was just that he'd seen so many up-and-down relationships that he'd come to believe he may never find true love. But, he realized, his fingers stopping on the guitar strings, he'd also seen the power of love heal.

The power of Javar and Whitney's love had brought them through the dark hours of their marriage. Khamil didn't doubt they'd remain happy forever.

Yes, Jessica had betrayed him, and as a result, he'd hardened his heart to love. But when he compared Monique to Jessica, there was no comparison. Thinking back, he recognized a self-centered side to Jessica, one he hadn't noticed until after their breakup. While with her, Khamil had been so enamored with her beauty that he'd hardly noticed her flaws.

And while Monique was a model and most definitely beautiful, she hardly seemed to know it. There was nothing about her that was conceited. There was nothing about her that was self-centered. Except for the fact that he'd been attracted to both women, Monique was nothing like Jessica.

He and Monique connected in a way that he and Jessica never had.

Annoyed with himself, Khamil stood. He returned the guitar to the closet. Now that he thought about it, really thought about it, he'd been wasting his pain and insecurity on someone who didn't deserve it. Jessica hadn't been the person he'd thought she was, and instead of conceding that he'd simply made an error in judgment, he'd let that negative relationship prevent him from being open to meeting someone else he could love.

But maybe he hadn't been open to letting that happen because the right person hadn't come along.

Until now.

Khamil climbed back into bed, propping his hands beneath his head. Was that it? Had it simply taken him all this time since high school to find the one person who was perfect for him?

And if Monique *was* the woman for him, how could he let fear and confusion get in the way of something that could potentially be wonderful?

He couldn't.

And he wouldn't.

It was high time he put the issues of distrust and fear as they pertained to Jessica where they belonged—in the past.

No one ever achieved anything worthwhile without taking a chance.

Twenty

As Monique got out of the tub, she heard the loud rapping on the door. Instantly, her stomach lurched with anticipation. It was late, after one in the morning, and she could think of only one person who'd be coming over this time of night.

Khamil.

Smiling, Monique grabbed a thick white towel, wrapped it around her body, then hustled to the door. Victor, the doorman who'd been on duty when she and Khamil had arrived here, had obviously recognized Khamil and let him back into the building.

At the door, Monique glimpsed through the peephole.

Her stomach sank to her knees.

Raymond!

"Open up, Monique," Raymond said. "I know you're in there."

Stepping back from the door, Monique looked around frantically. What should she do?

"C'mon, Monique."

God help her. "Raymond, I'm going to call the police."

"I don't think you want to do that."

"I don't want you here, Raymond."

"We need to talk."

"Go away."

"You want the truth about your mother, don't you? I have some answers for you."

Monique's hands were shaking. "I don't believe you, Raymond. Please, don't make me call the police. They already know you broke into my apartment and trashed my place."

"Actually, if you call them, they'll tell you they interviewed me. I have an alibi for the time your place was broken into."

Monique swallowed.

"They checked the tape, Monique. They didn't see me coming into your building."

Monique remained silent, and after a moment, Raymond said, "Come on. Do you really think I wouldn't be in custody if they had any evidence at all against me?"

"Why are you here?"

"There are some things you should know about your mother. Monique, I used to work with her."

A chill ran down Monique's arms and back. Raymond had worked with her mother? Why had he never said so before?

"I . . ."

"She was with the Snoe Agency on Sixth Avenue. It's since gone out of business."

"How do you know that?"

"Monique, for God's sake. Just open the door."

Monique whimpered, then bit her lip. The fact that Raymond knew even those details gave her hope that he was indeed telling the truth. But she didn't trust him, and she didn't want him in here.

Yet if he knew anything, she needed to hear what he had to say.

"Give me a second," Monique told him.

She scurried to the bedroom, where she slipped

into a robe. Then, she headed to the kitchen and took a butcher knife from a drawer.

She wasn't about to take any chances.

Monique opened the door, and Raymond quickly stepped into the apartment. He stopped short when he saw the knife Monique held.

"Holy, Monique."

She held the knife firmly ahead of him. "Look, I don't trust you. But I'm willing to hear you out. So tell me this news you came to tell me, then leave."

Raymond ground out a frustrated grunt. "Can I at least sit down?"

With the knife, Monique gestured to the living room.

"How did you get up here, by the way?" she asked once Raymond sat on her sofa.

"Victor let me up."

Victor. Damn. Monique hadn't spoken to him about her problems with Raymond, only Harry.

Raymond ran the back of his hand across his forehead, wiping away sweat that had popped out on his brow. "Do you have to . . . hold that knife?"

"Yes," Monique replied succinctly. "You have ten seconds to start talking before I start cutting."

Raymond held up both hands in surrender. "All right. I worked with your mother years ago. I photographed her on many occasions. I was fairly new to the business then, but I had a lot of contacts, and I was lucky enough to be able to work with her."

"What do you know about her murder?"

"I'm not sure."

"Get out."

"Will you wait a second?" Raymond's eyes implored Monique to listen. "What I'm saying is I can't be sure of who killed her, even if I have my suspicions."

"Keep talking."

"I never mentioned anything to you before, Monique, partly because I didn't want to tell you anything . . ." His eyes went skyward, as if searching for the right word. "Negative."

"What's that supposed to mean?"

"I know how much you adored your mother. I didn't want to burst that bubble."

Monique glared at Raymond. "Listen, if there's something you want to tell me, tell me. If not—"

"Your mother, for lack of a better word, was a flirt, Monique." Monique shot Raymond a startled gaze, and he continued. "She cheated on your father. More than once."

A ragged breath escaped her as she sat down on the sofa opposite Raymond. "God, please don't tell me what I think you're saying. . . ."

"No, I never slept with your mother. But not because she didn't try."

"God, no. . . ."

"Yeah. She tried to seduce me, Monique. More than once."

"And you never slept with her?"

"I was attracted to her, yes, but no, I didn't sleep with her."

Monique shot to her feet, paced a few steps. She stared at Raymond long and hard. "So, you dating me . . . what was that about? Your sick infatuation with my dead mother?"

"No," Raymond said, appalled. "Of course not."

"I don't know what to think," Monique said, her voice barely above a whisper.

"I fell for you because of you, Monique. Not because of your mother. I still care for you."

"You care so much that you cheated on me."

Raymond sighed. "I already told you, I'm sorry."

Monique waved a hand in front of her, dismissing the issue. "That's a moot point. Our relationship is over."

A frown played on Raymond's lips, but Monique held his gaze with a firm one. She wasn't about to back down on this issue.

"Anyway," Raymond said after a moment. "I'm not gonna lie. Your mother was an attractive woman, and I might have slept with her—if she hadn't been involved with one of my best friends."

Monique lowered herself back onto the sofa, a lump the size of a baseball forming in her chest. Who was her mother? She didn't know anymore.

"Like I said, that's the reason I never told you anything before. Because I knew it would hurt you. But your mother was involved with one of my colleagues and best friends. They'd been having an affair for several months."

Monique shut her eyes tight. How could this be true?

"He'd even been to your family's cottage in Canada."

Monique's eyes flew to Raymond's. "How do you know about the cabin?"

"I told you, Monique. My friend was having an affair with your mother. And . . . and he became obsessed with her."

"So he was Pooh-Bear?"

Raymond nodded slowly. "Yes. That's what she used to call him."

"Oh, God."

"Your mother tried to break things off when she realized he was getting too serious. That's when he started writing her letters, calling nonstop."

"If my mother knew it was him, how come the police don't know the identity of her stalker?"

"She didn't know it was him," Raymond explained. "He waited a while after she dumped him before starting to stalk her. He was trying to scare her. He just couldn't let go."

Monique stood and walked toward the living room window. Her mind was racing with so many questions, she was as breathless as if she'd just run a marathon. She remembered her father's question about whether or not she was prepared to learn the truth about her mother, no matter what.

Nausea churned in her stomach. All she'd wanted was to learn the identity of her mother's killer. She hadn't been prepared to learn this.

She turned.

And screamed.

Raymond stood mere inches from her.

Quick as lightning, he grabbed the wrist that held the knife.

Adrenaline took over. Monique fought for dear life to hold onto the knife while Raymond twisted her hand, trying to make her drop it. She screamed as she struggled. Raymond was stronger than she, and her wrist was throbbing with pain from how hard he was twisting it.

But she wouldn't let go.

Couldn't.

"You're even more beautiful than your mother," Raymond whispered in a voice so cool, you'd never know he was actually struggling with her. "Oh, God. You don't know how badly I want you."

Grunting, Monique shoved a shoulder into Raymond's chest. The effort paid off, and she stumbled as her body went free of his grip.

But Raymond recovered quickly, then walked slowly toward her.

"It doesn't have to be like this, Monique. If you'll

love me, the way it's supposed to be, we can have everything."

"You're deranged." Monique took a few steps backward, rounding herself around the coffee table. All the while, she kept the knife aimed at him. If he made a move for her, she wouldn't hesitate to stab him.

Help . . . me. . . .

The memory of her mother dying in her arms hit Monique with such velocity that she actually shook. But she didn't stop moving. The phone was close, just a few feet away. If she could reach it . . .

Raymond's eyes flitted from her face to beyond her shoulder. She knew he'd read her thoughts.

He lunged for her. Without thinking, Monique threw the knife at him, then dove for the phone. She couldn't risk him overpowering her and using the knife against her.

She knocked the receiver off the hook and hit the first programmed button her fingers could meet.

"Help!" she cried. "Please come quickly. Raymond Stuart, he's a photographer—"

Raymond's eyes grew wide with alarm. He stood over her for a moment, then quickly retreated and darted out of the apartment.

The moment he was gone, Monique sprung to her feet. She charged for the door, quickly locking and bolting it.

Then she slumped down the length of the door. She couldn't stop the tears.

"Oh, God. Thank you. Thank you." Not even knowing whom she'd dialed or if she'd reached anyone, Monique had acted as though her call had gone to the police. It had been enough to scare Raymond off.

The phone. She had to call the police. Monique

got to her feet and hurried back into the living room. She grabbed the receiver and held it to her ear.

"Hello?" she heard.

A sob escaped her. "Aunt Sophie?"

"Monique. My God, what's wrong?"

"Oh, Aunt Sophie." Monique broke down. Then she told her aunt what had happened.

"I'm on my way. Make some chamomile tea. When I get there, we'll call the police."

"I'll call them now."

Aunt Sophie hesitated, then said, "I'd like to be there with you when you make the call, sweetheart. I know you've been confused about a lot of things for a long time, and it's time you got some answers."

"Aunt Sophie?" Monique asked, perplexed. But she'd already hung up.

Monique stared at the receiver for several seconds. In twenty-four hours, her life had turned completely upside down. Never in a million years would she have expected to learn what she had about her mother.

Why had her mother cheated on her father? Despite her parents' arguments, Monique had known that her father adored her mother.

So many questions. She wanted answers.

Monique stood and went to the door. She glanced through the peephole. Satisfied that Raymond was gone, she went to the kitchen to make some tea, as her aunt had suggested.

But in the kitchen, she leaned a hip against the counter and closed her eyes. Her stomach was too queasy even for tea. Besides, tea wouldn't do anything for her. Only answers would.

"Raymond," she said sadly as she headed back to the living room. "How could you do this?"

Monique sat down on the sofa, burying her face in her hands. After a second, her head whipped up. Her heart suddenly beat so fast, she thought it might explode.

Had Raymond killed her mother?

He had to have killed her, the same way he'd planned to kill her tonight. The pieces fit together . . . so why didn't it feel right?

Monique went to the phone and picked up the receiver. She dialed the number to her father's home in Florida. It rang and rang until the machine came on. She hung up and dialed again.

This time, her father answered after the second ring. His voice was groggy as he said, "Hello?"

"Daddy."

"Monique." Pause. "It's nearly two in the morning. Why are you calling so late?"

"Dad, someone tried to kill me tonight."

After her father's startled gasp, Monique filled him in on the night's events.

"My God," her father said. "This man worked with your mother years ago? He's the one who killed her?"

"I thought that," Monique said slowly. "But I'm not so sure anymore."

"Why?"

"Daddy, I need for you to tell me the truth. No matter how awful it might be. No matter what may have happened that night, I'll always love you. I want you to know that."

There was a pause, then Lucas said, "Are you asking me if I killed your mother?"

"Did you?"

Lucas didn't respond right away, and Monique's

heart dropped to her knees. God, no. All this time, she'd so desperately wanted to believe in her father's innocence.

"No," her father finally said.

A sigh of relief oozed out of Monique. Her father's tone was soft, but it didn't waver, and Monique knew without a doubt that he was telling the truth.

"But you knew she was having an affair."

"Yes."

"Why didn't you tell me?"

"I didn't want anything . . ." His voice cracked. "I didn't want to ruin the image you had of your mother."

It was love Monique heard in her father's voice, love she heard among his tears. And her heart spilled over with love for him then, appreciating the fact that he'd done all he could to protect her from a truth that would have hurt her.

But Monique knew there was more to the situation than that. So she said, "Even after what Mom did, you still loved her."

"Yes," Lucas said sadly. "I love her still. She was my life."

The tears she heard in her father's voice brought tears to her own eyes. Her mother had had a wonderful man in Lucas Savard. Why hadn't she appreciated that?

Sadly, Monique realized that she would never know the answer to that question. Her mother had taken those answers to her grave.

"I love you, sweetheart," Lucas said. "You're all I have left of Julia, and I don't want to lose you. Please, please, take care of yourself."

"I will, Daddy." A mixture of happiness and sadness swirled within Monique. While she'd always known in her heart that her father couldn't have killed her mother, she hadn't quite understood the depth of his love for her. She understood now.

"Listen, Daddy. Go back to sleep. We'll talk in the morning."

"Okay," he said.

He sounded so frail, and Monique was reminded of life's cruelest lesson. She wouldn't have her father forever. "I'll visit you soon. Maybe even next week."

"I'd like that," Lucas said. "I miss you."

"I miss you, too. And I love you."

"I love you, too."

Hearing a smile in her father's voice brought happiness to Monique. Yeah, she'd go see him as soon as she could.

She ended the call, but held the receiver to her heart for several minutes. She couldn't feel any more love for her father than she felt at that moment. He was such a special man.

Her mind wandered to Khamil. He was a special man, too. He'd been by her side during this whole ordeal, never casting judgment against her mother or her father, instead lending her a shoulder to cry on.

She wanted to call him, but she was afraid. She was in love with him, and wanted to share things with him for that reason. But could she deal with the fact that he might only want to be her friend?

Now wasn't the time to think about that. All her life, she'd carried the heavy burden of what had happened that horrible night on her own, and it had felt good to have Khamil carry some of that load with her. He'd not only shown her that she didn't have to be strong all the time, he'd offered to be strong for her.

Yes, she'd call him. She needed him now.

The phone rang twice and Monique was about to

hang up, figuring Khamil was sleeping. But he answered.

"Hello?"

"Hey. Khamil. You sound wide awake."

"I couldn't sleep." Pause. "Are you okay?"

Thinking of the night's events, Monique was suddenly overwhelmed. "No. I'm not."

"I'm on my way."

Before she could say good-bye, Monique heard the dial tone.

Yeah, Khamil was a very special man. A special man, just like her father.

Twenty-one

"Sure," Monique told Victor, the doorman. "Send him up."

"Will do."

"Oh, and, Victor," Monique quickly said before he could hang up. "I'm expecting someone else. Khamil Jordan. When he arrives, please send him up."

Monique stood and strolled to the kitchen. Her nerves finally settling, she was now ready for some tea. She was glad to know that her cousin was on his way up and that Khamil was on his way over. She didn't feel alone.

Monique filled the kettle with water, then plugged it in the wall.

There was a knock on the door, and she hurried to answer it. Opening it, a smile spread on her face. "Daniel."

"Hey, cuz." He gave her a brief hug, then stepped into the apartment. His expression grew serious. "What the hell happened?"

"God." Monique wrapped her arms around her torso. "Raymond. He's a nutcase. He came here with some cock-and-bull story and I . . . I let him in." She explained to her cousin how she'd gotten a knife before doing so, how that knife had given her a false sense of security.

"I told you what you were doing was dangerous."

"I know. Everyone did. The thing is, I got involved with Raymond before the police reopened my mother's murder case. This would have happened one way or another."

Daniel nodded grimly. "Well, at least you're okay."

"Yeah." Thinking of the reality of how differently the night's events could have played out, Monique shuddered. "I've got the kettle on. I'm making some tea. Would you like a cup?"

"Sure."

"I'm having mint tea. Is that okay with you?"

"Mint tea sounds great."

Monique started for the kitchen. "Take a seat and make yourself comfortable. When I come back out, we'll talk."

In the kitchen, Monique busied herself with putting tea bags in mugs, then filling the mugs with water.

"You want sugar?" she asked.

"Two spoons, please."

Monique did as instructed, then brought both mugs into the living room. She handed Daniel his, then sat on the love seat across from where he sat on the sofa.

"So," Daniel said. "This Raymond guy, he killed your mother."

Monique brought the mug to her lips and cautiously took a sip. It was still too hot. "Actually, I'm not sure he did."

Daniel's eyes shot up. "You're not?"

"I don't know," Monique said, shaking her head. "It doesn't feel right."

"The guy tried to kill you. He was obsessed with your mother, and now with you."

"I know, but . . ." What was it that was bothering

her? She couldn't place her finger on it. All she knew was that her intuition said Raymond hadn't killed her mother.

"So he was Pooh-Bear?"

Pooh-Bear.

"Don't tell me you're still going to continue this crazy quest of yours, Monique."

"Until I'm sure Raymond killed my mother, you can't honestly expect me to give up now."

"Monique, what's wrong with you?"

As her cousin voiced his disapproval, Monique's mind wandered. Pooh-Bear. Why did that ring a bell?

"Where's your mother?" Monique suddenly asked Daniel. "She said she was coming." She brought the mug to her lips.

"She's dead."

The mug fell to the carpet, hot liquid splashing everywhere.

His eyes turning black, Daniel leveled his gaze on her. He placed his mug on the coffee table, then stood. Horrified, Monique stared at him.

"What did you say?" she asked.

"My mother is dead."

"Dead?" A moan fell from Monique's lips. "My God, why didn't you say something?"

Daniel started toward her, the coldest expression she'd ever seen on his face.

"You should have stopped this when I told you, Monique."

"Why do they call you Pooh-Bear, Uncle Richard?"

She heard the question in her mind so clearly, she wondered how she had ever forgotten it.

"You?" she managed between ragged breaths.

"Your mother was a whore, Monique. She was a whore who slept with as many men as she could. But

when she tried to take my father from us, I had to
stop her."

"Oh, my God." Monique shot to her feet.

"My mother never let me forget it. Every day, she
told me how your mother had ruined her life, how
she thought she was literally dying of a broken heart
because of what she'd done. I thought . . ." Daniel
paused as pain flashed across his face. "I thought I
was losing my mother. Do you know that I found
her unconscious in the bathroom? She'd overdosed
on pills, Monique. She tried to kill herself, because
of what your mother did to her."

Monique was so light-headed, she thought she
might pass out. "What are you saying, Daniel?"

"Do you believe that after all these years, after my
mother practically made me kill your mother, she
wanted to come clean?" His lips pulled in a taut line.
"I'm not going to jail, Monique. Not for a whore."

Oh, my God, oh, my God. Think, Monique. Think!
"Daniel, no one's sending you to jail. You were young
when you committed the crime."

"I was eighteen, Monique. Legally an adult."

Slowly, Monique took a step backward. She didn't
recognize the Daniel who stood before her, and she
had no clue what he was capable of. "You need help,
Daniel. We can get you help."

"That's what my mother said. Right before I killed
her."

Monique threw a hand to her mouth as she gasped.

"She was going to come over here and tell you
everything. I couldn't let her do that."

He was crazy. If he'd killed her mother and his
own, surely he would kill her.

Monique whirled around, darting into the kitchen.
Daniel gave chase.

Monique screamed when his fingers dug into her

shoulders. He spun her around and slammed her against the wall, ramming his forearm against her windpipe.

"Please, Daniel." Monique gasped for air. "Please don't do this."

Daniel's body pressed her against the wall with a quick shove and again, Monique screamed. A moment later, when she saw him fall to the floor, she looked up, stunned.

And saw Khamil.

It took her only a second to realize that Khamil was actually there and not a figment of her imagination. A relieved cry escaping her, she jumped into his arms.

"Oh, Khamil." She wrapped her arms tightly around his neck.

"Monique." He squeezed her hard, as if he wanted to meld their bodies together.

"Oh, thank God you came."

Khamil pulled back to look at her. "Are you okay?"

Monique managed a jerky nod. "Yeah. I'm okay now."

Khamil held her to his body again, and Monique closed her eyes, savoring the wonderful feel of him. After a moment, she told him how Raymond had showed up first.

Monique looked down at her cousin's motionless body. "Is he . . ."

"He's out cold, and he will be for a while. A move I learned in martial arts." A sly grin spread on Khamil's face.

"You're a man of many talents, aren't you?"

"So I'm told."

Monique pressed her head to Khamil's chest. She was safe. The nightmare was finally over.

"Damn, girl," Khamil said after a long moment.

"You were going to get yourself killed before I had the chance to tell you that I love you?"

"It's been a night of close calls, but—" Stopping abruptly, Monique tilted her head and met Khamil's eyes. "What did you just say?"

Khamil met her gaze, steady and strong. Then a small smile spread on his face. "I think I just said that I love you."

Monique's heart thumped erratically. Did Khamil mean what he'd just said, or had his words merely been a reaction to this serious situation?

"And . . . do you?" Monique asked. "Love me?"

His smile grew until it was a wide grin. "Yeah," he replied, nodding. "I do."

A squeal erupted in Monique's throat.

"I've never met anyone quite like you, Monique. And until I did, I figured I just might spend the rest of my days as a bachelor." His hand found her face, and he trailed his fingers along her cheek. "But I know now that I don't want that. I want you."

"Oh."

"When I heard your scream, then saw you pressed up against the wall . . . God, I was so afraid I was going to lose you before I ever had the chance to love you."

Happy, Monique squealed again. "This isn't a dream? You're not just saying this?"

Khamil shook his head. "You know how well we connected, Monique. We found something rare, and I don't want to lose that." He paused, then narrowed his eyes as he looked down at her. "Wait a second. I'm telling you all this, yet I don't know how you feel about me."

Monique angled her head to the side and framed Khamil's face. "Yes, you do. A connection this strong couldn't be one-sided." She paused, happy tears filling her eyes. "I love you, Khamil Jordan."

He smiled again, then lowered his lips to hers. He kissed her until they were both breathless.

"Will you marry me?"

Monique's eyes registered shock.

"Why wait?" Khamil asked. "When you find something that's real, why let it slip away?"

Why indeed? And Monique knew that Khamil was special, rare. He was a good man, a passionate man, just like her father.

So she said, "Yes. Oh, Khamil. Yes!"

Khamil held her to him, lifting her feet off the ground. And as he spun her around, Monique couldn't stop giggling, knowing that her dream of finding that one man who would love her forever had finally come true.

Epilogue

"Wow," Javar said.

"I know." Khamil had just finished telling his brother about all that had transpired a few days ago. Even now, it seemed too incredible to be true.

"After what happened with Mom and Whitney, I figured I was the only one in the family who was going to see this much drama," Javar commented.

Khamil looked to Monique's naked, sleeping form on the bed beside him, bathed in the morning sunlight. The sight did his heart good. At last she was getting some decent rest, once and for all putting the whole nightmare of her past behind her.

"Yeah, who would have thought?" Khamil said after a moment, answering Javar. "Hopefully there'll be no more drama like this."

"From now on, just diaper drama and feedings in the middle of the night, right?" Javar laughed. "Like what I have to look forward to?"

"Hey, sounds good to me," Khamil replied.

There was a pause; then Javar said, "Man, I can't believe I'm hearing you talk like this, little brother."

"Hmm." Once, Khamil wouldn't have pictured it, either. Now, the idea was actually appealing. And compared to stalkers and other psychos, diapers and feedings would be welcome—when the time came.

In the days since the attack on Monique's life, a
lot had happened. Both Daniel and Raymond had
been arrested, Daniel for two counts of murder and
Raymond for stalking and attempted murder. Daniel
indeed had murdered his own mother to keep her
from telling the horrible truth about the past; she'd
played on young Daniel's emotions, making Julia
Savard out to be a threat to the family because she
was sleeping with Richard. Daniel, who'd been
chronically depressed for years, was afraid he'd lose
his mother because of Julia, so he'd killed Julia. In
his mind, he'd been doing the right thing, hoping
to save his own mother, who'd been withdrawn and
suicidal because of her husband's affair. Now, Daniel
would no doubt spend the better part of his life behind bars. It was a sad situation all around.

Raymond had admitted to police that he'd broken
into Monique's apartment and trashed it, leaving the
rose petals and vandalizing the wall. But as disturbing
as all that was, Monique actually received some peace
of mind from Raymond when he admitted that he'd
lied about her mother's character. Yes, Raymond had
worked with her years ago. He'd been infatuated with
her then, but they'd never had an affair, and she
hadn't had an affair with any other photographer.
However, she'd considered Raymond a friend and
had confessed to him that she'd made a mistake and
gotten involved with her husband's younger brother.
Raymond had always held out hope that by being
there for her, she'd come to realize that she loved
him. To that measure, he'd begun stalking her, hoping in his sick, twisted way to once again show her
that he was there for her, that she could count on
him to protect her, and that as a result she would
come to love him.

Years later, that infatuation had carried over to

Julia's daughter. Once again, he'd resorted to head games and manipulation in an attempt to control the new object of his desire. He'd succeeded in dating Monique, but was always afraid he'd lose her. And when he'd cheated on her, he had actually hoped to make her insecure enough that she would cling to him—all in a bizarre effort to keep her. When that failed, he'd begun stalking her with letters, the way he had stalked her mother, hoping that he'd realize she needed a man—him—in her life, to feel safe.

"So," Javar said, a smile in his voice. "You're really going to take the plunge?"

"Yep." Khamil trailed his fingers along Monique's spine, bringing them to a rest in the groove of her back. Stirring, she moaned softly. "In less than a week, my bachelor days will be over."

"It's about time," Javar quipped playfully.

"It's kind of amazing," Khamil said. "You search all your life for the right person, not knowing if you'll ever find her. Then bam, just like that, she walks into your life."

"That's the way it was with me and Whitney. I knew the moment I saw her." Javar paused. "And I thank God every day that we worked our problems out."

"I hear you."

"Well, I can't wait to see Monique again, the one woman who's done what we all thought impossible— stolen your heart."

Khamil chuckled. "You will. We'll head to Chicago after the honeymoon. And you know we'll be there when Whitney has the baby."

"You better," Javar told his brother. "Hey, we found out she's having a little girl. And Samona is having a boy. Man, this is gonna be fun."

"I'll bet." Khamil glanced at Monique. He wondered if she wanted to start a family soon. Well, he knew they'd at least have fun trying.

"How's Jamaica?" Javar asked.

"Beautiful," Khamil crooned. "Wish you were here."

"I'm sure you do."

Khamil chuckled.

Monique stirred, turning onto her back. Opening her eyes, she smiled at him. "Who is it?" she asked softly.

"My brother," Khamil replied. He brought a hand to her breast, tweaking a nipple. Monique giggled.

"Okay, little brother," Javar said. "Sounds like you're busy. Call me after you've jumped the broom."

"Don't think I'll do it?"

"Hey, with you, I have to see it to believe it."

"Believe it," Khamil said. " 'Cause my bachelor days are over." He winked at Monique. "And speaking of that, my future wife beckons."

"All right. Later."

Khamil hung up the phone, then slid across the bed to Monique. He took her naked body in his arms, then nuzzled his nose against her neck.

She giggled. "Stop!" She fought to get away from him, but Khamil didn't relent. "Come on. You know I'm ticklish Khamil!"

Chortling, Khamil finally let up. He brought his mouth to her lips, kissing her briefly but passionately. Then he pulled back and gazed down at her. "So, Mrs. Jordan-to-be. What shall we do? You feel up to some snorkeling today? Or sailing maybe?"

"Actually." Monique brought her hands to Khamil's chest. "The future Mrs. Jordan isn't feeling very well." She flashed a playful pout. "She thinks she's going to have to spend the entire day in bed, being taken care of by the very handsome Mr. Jordan—whom, by the way, she can't wait to marry."

Khamil arched an eyebrow. "Is that so?"

Monique raised her head, stopping her lips a fraction of an inch from his. "Uh-huh. Think you're up to the task?"

Khamil gave her a sexy smile. "I think so."

" 'Cause if you don't do a good job of taking care of me, I may not be able to marry you."

"In that case . . ." Khamil draped an arm across her waist, then flicked his tongue over her ear. "I'd better start taking care of you right now."

"Ooh, I love a man who listens to me."

Khamil skimmed his lips across her cheek. "Hey, I'll do my part to make sure you're . . . *well.*"

"Mmm." Monique ran a hand over Khamil's bald head. "I'm liking this already."

Khamil brushed his nose over hers. "No doubt you are."

Monique wrapped her arms tightly around his neck. "Come here."

"Oh, baby. . . ." Khamil did as told, settling on top of her.

He was liking married life already.

He wasn't going to miss his bachelor days. Not one bit.

More Sizzling Romance From
Brenda Jackson